THE VAMPIRE OF SIAM

JIM NEWPORT

Encyclopocalypse Publications
www.encyclopocalypse.com

ISBN: 978-1-960721-30-3

Cover formatting and design by Sean Duregger
Vampire of Siam logo and branding designed by Ben Howard of Eqco.one
Internal formatting by Sean Duregger
Author photograph: Anthony Edwards

www.vampireofsiam.com

BOOKS BY JIM NEWPORT

The Vampire of Siam

Ramonne: The Return of The Vampire of Siam

The Reckoning: A Tale of The Vampire of Siam

Chasing Jimi

Tinsel Town

The Siamese Connection

A Dark Christmas

PRAISE FOR JIM NEWPORT

THE VAMPIRE OF SIAM

"Grand Guignol entertainment…good for nibbling on the beach."

— JAMES ECKARDT, THE NATION.

"Chilling and morbidly hilarious. Newport's intimate knowledge of the Far East makes this an ultra-realistic journey into terror."

— PULITZER PRIZE NOMINATED AUTHOR CHRIS BUNCH.

"Well-researched, engrossing, smart and sexy. A graveyard smash."

— BOBBY 'BORIS' PICKETT, SINGER-SONGWRITER: THE MONSTER MASH.

Rating: 5 stars

— JOHN WALSH, MANGO SAUCE.

RAMONNE

"Newport retains, from his first novel, a sharp sense of place for modern Bangkok. This is the trendy Bangkok of the Emporium Suites, the skytrain, the Q Bar, the Bed Supperclub."

— THE NATION.

"Newport artfully adapts the vampire legend into a Mekong cocktail of surprises."

— CHRISTOPHER G. MOORE.

THE RECKONING

"Newport's novels succeed in their purpose: they entertain."

— THE NATION.

"The books are rich in cinematic imagery...and fascinating details of Thai history."

— THAILAND TATLER.

CHASING JIMI

"Did you miss the 1960s? This funny yet loving and respectful adventure mystery will take you back."

— JERRY HOPKINS, AUTHOR OF THE DOORS: NO ONE HERE GETS OUT ALIVE.

"Newport has gone from the vault of the dead to the electrifying life of Jimi Hendrix. If you can remember Woodstock, you will enjoy this book."

— LANG REID, PATTAYA MAIL.

TINSEL TOWN

"It moves like a runaway asteroid."

— TIM HALLINAN, BESTSELLING AUTHOR OF THE POKE RAFFERTY SERIES (SET IN BANGKOK).

"Tinsel Town is the best introduction-to-Hollywood novel I've ever read."

— DAVID GILER, PRODUCER/WRITER OF THE FILMS ALIEN, UNDISPUTED, MYRA BRECKINRIDGE AND MANY MORE.

THE SIAMESE CONNECTION

"Jim Newport is a writer with great skills. Non-stop, hold your breath action. A true thriller. "

— LANG REID, PATTAYA MAIL

"Newport clearly knows Bangkok…An easy read."

— BERNARD TRINK, BANGKOK POST.

ACKNOWLEDGMENTS

My thanks to Pacharee for introducing me to the wonders of Thailand; Tim Young, Patrick "Shrimp" Gauvain, and Nick Palevsky for opening the doors; Khun Yui for the research; the late David Jameson; Hubert & Manat for providing the sanctuary I needed to write this book, and Rich Baker for making the book a reality.

THE VAMPIRE OF SIAM

VoS 1

1

———

Ramonne moved effortlessly down the deserted *soi*. At 4:00 a.m., Bangkok's infamous Patpong Road, home to go-go bars and live sex shows, was almost as empty as the great Sahara. He brushed off the approaches of the few *katoeys* who lurked in the shadows of the street that only two hours before had been a reveling cornucopia of sinners.

Now it was quiet, except for the forklifts that raced from Surawong to Silom Road. Like freight trains they sped north, loaded with the iron frames and tattered canvas awnings that were used to construct the demented Disneyland of counterfeit goods stalls that filled the street each evening. They raced south empty, their metal arms open and eager for the gathering.

A single white headlight drove down the center of the street, deliberately aiming at Ramonne's arrogant swagger. It was a game that one of the forklift drivers, a shirtless youth, played with the *farangs* to ease the boredom of the nightly task of tearing down and packing away the stalls. Ramonne was not amused. As the vehicle swerved at the last moment, he spat viscous, acid-filled phlegm at the boy. It burned his skin, and he lost control and crashed into the shuttered facade of the Superstar bar.

Ramonne smiled and strutted on without a backward glance. He remembered a time when Krung Thep pulsated with life all night long. But of course he also remembered a time when the red-light district was very different, when there were no motor cars to pollute the glorious, jasmine-scented air. A time when gilded royal barges bedecked with golden lanterns glided silently through the *klongs*, their only sound the titillating laughter of the beautiful courtesans within. *Ah, those were the nights.*

Ramonne settled into his usual booth at the Tip Top Café. The soot-stained, naked fluorescent lights cast shadows into the corners of the dingy refuge, at this hour the only place open to get a drink or a miserable meal. Around Ramonne the not-yet-dead mingled with the almost-dead and the soon to be-dead. A Thai Elvis from the Music Bar, his ancient eyes hidden behind trademark, oversized shades, sat with a group of customers. A little girl, probably no more than eight years old, wandered the room, her wide eyes pleading for someone to buy the wilting roses or chewing gum she hawked in the bars each night.

Home.

Ramonne spied Kimchi sat in a booth at the back, eating her noodles with chopsticks, her once blonde hair, now red, tumbling across her face. Her roommates, Lek and Noi, cackled inanely about men and money.

Ramonne grabbed her with his eyes. It was so fucking easy. He'd done it, what…? Ten thousand times…? A hundred thousand? They'd lock eyes, she'd blush—as much as a dark-skinned Isaan girl could—he'd nod, and she would shift uncomfortably in her seat. He'd motion to the empty booth across from him. She'd make an excuse to her girlfriends.

The deal was done.

2

———

Bangkok. The second year of the new millennium. *God, what a difference a year makes.*

Martin Larue negotiated the cracked pavement, trying to maintain his balance in front of the steel and glass tower that housed the offices of the *Bangkok Times,* one of the main English-language newspapers in the kingdom. He was home, but that didn't mean he would stay. Martin's feet never stayed any place very long. Wealthy beyond measure—the result of a well-endowed trust fund—all Martin needed was a visa every thirty days, and Don Muang Airport's easy international access. It seemed that his only real problem was answering the question: "What do you do?" Travel for travel's sake wasn't a satisfactory answer to most who asked. So he had taken his fondness for cinema and his connections at the *Times* to their logical conclusion. He was a "film critic" for the paper's weekend supplement. This gave him easy access to cushy press passes at obscure film festivals in mountain resorts around the globe. It also gave his ramblings a destination. If he was off to a film festival, his life had purpose. He was on a mission. He would record his thoughts, and the *Times* would publish. That was the plan, and Lord it was working beautifully.

That was until the day Dam Prakasan took over as managing editor of the *Times*. Martin's girlfriend Daeng, who answered all his calls, was the first to tell him his presence was required at the office. An office he'd never even been to.

"What the hell do they need *me* out there for?" he complained. Martin's contributions were always sent via e-mail.

Daeng had shrugged.

"I contribute my stuff for *free*. Why would I want to schlep out to their lousy offices?"

But Martin found himself on the skytrain the next day, getting off at Mor Chit, the furthermost point, and then taking another thirty-minute taxi ride to the new economically-viable-but-couldn't-be-further-from-town offices of the *Times*, riding the elevator to the sixteenth floor in complete silence, and holding in his uttermost contempt for the working class.

––––––

"*Ah*, Martin, what a pleasure to finally meet you. Please have a seat." Managing Editor Prakasan seemed over-enthusiastic as he ushered Martin into his office. "Coffee…?" He nodded to the young woman who had appeared in the doorway.

Martin looked around the cluttered office. He often worried about finding a chair that was capable of accommodating his ever-expanding American butt, but he saw a Chinese rosewood affair that appeared stable enough.

"*Kor Nam plao, khrap*," Martin replied with barely a trace of accent. A life free of responsibilities had allowed him to master seven languages. As the girl departed, he mopped his still dripping brow. He had yet to master the Thai ability to remain cool and dry in the steam-bath environment.

Managing Editor Prakasan returned to his seat. "I have been making your acquaintance through the absorption of your past submissions."

What the hell does that mean? Martin puzzled, until he saw

Prakasan leafing through a file of clippings.

"I'm particularly fond of your voluminous critique of the zeitgeist masterpiece *The Adventures of Baron Munchausen.*"

Martin tried to put the pompous, college-level piece out of his mind. He cringed when he recalled his comparison of the Baron's sidekick, a flatulent dwarf, to an Olympic gymnast, enormously popular at the time.

Prakasan waved the clipping. "Pure poetry. I salute you, sir."

Martin squirmed. The *Munchausen* review was one of his first, and he'd delivered a tome of close to 10,000 words. That the *Times* had chosen to publish even a greatly condensed version was a surprise.

But he liked to think that his recent forays into the realm of cinematic journalism were worth the paper they were printed on. He was particularly proud of the slam he had recently given to Hollywood's latest computer-game-come-to-life mega-hit: *Lara Croft Tomb Raider* was headlined as LOAD OF CRAP TIME WASTER.

Prakasan continued: "But, judging by what I've digested of your recent gourmand, you've grown a bit stale. It's time for a change, Martin. Shake it up. Rattle the old gray matter."

What in the world is he babbling about?

Martin was relieved as the girl brought in his iced water.

"I want you to write a human interest story. A complete diversion from your cinematic dissertations. Something to touch the masses. The heart and souls of the proletariat."

"No offense, but I don't exactly *relate* to the working class."

"Precisely, Martin. That's your problem. You need to get your hands dirty."

"Why?"

Why, indeed. Martin had avoided *real* work like the plague. The mere thought of it repulsed him.

"Martin. You are, dare I say, out of touch. Even a film critic needs a grounded perspective on his audience. But you have the literary skills for such an undertaking. Therefore I've arranged for you to go on a 'ride-along' program with the Bangrak police. Lieutenant-Colonel Boonsong will be your *chargé d'affaires*, and I think you'll find it quite stimulating."

"What?" Martin sat up in his seat. "Now see here, I only write for your rag as a hobby. I have no interest, human or otherwise, in delving into the murk and mire of Bangrak in the back of a police car. Why me? Don't you have experienced local journalists to cover this type of thing."

But Managing Editor Prakasan had taken a shine to Martin for some reason. "Well, Martin. It's the foreigner's perspective that we're after. The local journalists aren't quite as…forthright, shall we say." He stood and walked to the large window behind his desk. He motioned and Martin moved next to him.

The view was spectacular. The city of almost ten million had suffered a construction boom in the nineties that had transformed its once low-rise charm to a concrete hell of skyscrapers and bizarre architecture. In the frenzy to build—condos, malls, offices, anything—the banks overlooked the necessity for finding purchasers for these symbols of the new economic dream, or even of having paying tenants. As a result—when the economic bubble splattered all over the incompetent finance sector—the city was left with a riot of buildings that were incomplete or unoccupied. Like whale carcasses rotting on a filthy beach.

The 35-story Golden Tower that was directly adjacent to the *Times*, was entirely vacant. From the sixteenth floor up, it didn't even have glass in the windows.

"Scary, isn't it?" Prakasan mused. "Man's race for riches can cause such monumental blunders."

Martin stared out at the surreal sight of swirling little eddies of paper and debris being carried from floor to floor. They moved aimlessly, drifting like gliders on thermal updrafts.

Like me.

Martin now pondered Prakasan's offer. Perhaps it wasn't

such a bad idea. After all, his existence *had* become jaded, and he was in the mood for a new kick.

"When would this little excursion take place?"

Prakasan smiled. "At your convenience, Martin. All you need do is call Lieutenant-Colonel Boonsong. The matter is arranged."

Reluctantly, Martin accepted the official police business card that a now beaming Prakasan extended.

"I'll think about it," he replied as he exited.

What the hell.

3

____

Lieutenant-Colonel Boonsong was an archetype—thin and wiry with a dark-brown uniform so tight it might as well have been body paint. He showed no trace of emotion as Martin entered the Bangrak Police Station on Thanon Naret. He put a fresh clip into his 9-mm Beretta, and snapped the pistol into his holster before he acknowledged Martin's presence.

"Mr. Larue." Boonsong looked up, then motioned to a man at least ten years his junior, yet otherwise identical in uniform and physique, but sporting a thin pencil mustache. "Sergeant Thamarat. He will lead us tonight on our patrol."

Thamarat snapped his heels and gave a smart salute. Martin was about to return it when Boonsong intervened. "Mr. Larue. Are you ready?"

"Ready as I'll ever be."

"Sign here please, and we can go." Boonsong presented a four-page document, single-spaced, in Thai. Martin _could_ have read it, but it would have taken most of the night. He recognized Managing Editor Prakasan's signature next to where Boonsong was pointing, and so he signed.

"Let's go."

Their vehicle was a white '99 Toyota Corolla with full light bar, parked directly in front of the functional four-story police station. Sergeant Thamarat was the driver. Martin got into the rear, and immediately noted the lack of door handles. Between the officers in the front was a black computer keyboard and a 12-inch screen. Sergeant Thamarat switched on the computer before starting the ignition.

They pulled out of Naret into Surawong, heading west toward the river.

"Bangrak is a triangle-shaped area in the middle of the financial district," Boonsong remarked. "It includes five foreign embassies, three hospitals, three colleges, six banks, and the Patpong night market. But of course you know all this, Mr. Larue. You're a long-term Bangkok resident—an 'Old Thai Hand' as they say."

Martin eyed the back of Boonsong's head. "I've spent a fair amount of time in the kingdom," he offered.

"Fifteen years is more than a 'fair amount' of time, my friend," Boonsong concurred, switching to Thai.

Fuck. So much for trying to remain anonymous.

Martin had decided long ago that anonymity was definitely a benefit in traveling through life. Particularly when it came to dealing with the law. Not that he had anything to hide. But wealth alone was reason enough to remain anonymous, and he was certain he didn't want Lieutenant-Colonel Boonsong to know too much about his personal life.

"Why do you travel so much, Mr. Larue?"

"For my work. You know, as a film critic. I go to a lot of film festivals."

"*Former* film critic, according to Khun Prakasan. Must be tiresome…the constant unknown nature of living out of a suitcase. I like to wake in the middle of the night and know exactly where my bathroom is."

"I find travel stimulating," Martin countered.

"Well, hopefully tonight's journey will provide some stimulation for your new journalistic ventures."

"Hopefully."

The radio crackled to life and Sergeant Thamarat responded. The voice on the other end told of an accident on Rama IV. Thamarat replied that they were on their way. He flicked on the siren and the red lights, and they turned into Soi Pramot and back into Surawong Road, effectively executing a 180-degree change of direction against the one-way traffic. Martin held his breath. He'd never traveled east before on Surawong. He winced and gripped his shoulder restraint as *tuk-tuks*, taxis, and lorries made last-minute swerves to avoid a head-on collision with the speeding police vehicle.

"We're on our way to the scene of an accident. A motorcycle and a car have had an encounter. I hope it has less than the usual result."

Martin breathed a sigh of relief as they reached Rama IV Road and made a legal right turn, joining the traffic heading southwest to Silom Road.

Just before Silom they saw the carnage.

A mangled, hot-pink Yamaha speedster lay in the entry to the Dusit Thani Hotel. It's former rider, a young man, lay ten meters away, his body bent at an impossible angle. Blood, and other things, ran from a crack that evenly split his skull in two. His helmet was still strapped to the rear of his crumpled motorcycle.

A uniformed policeman with a white helmet was questioning the visibly shaken driver of a black Mercedes parked in the center of the intersection. Boonsong and Thamarat exited the car, both either forgetting or choosing not to open the rear door for Martin, who stared as the flashing lights cast red strobe patterns on the macabre scene.

Boonsong moved to the driver of the Mercedes, a man in a black business suit who seemed greatly relieved to see the colonel. He stumbled and almost fell. Boonsong caught him and helped him regain his balance.

The man *waied* Boonsong like a long lost friend. Boonsong

took out a small pad and jotted a few notes. Within minutes they *waied* each other again, and the uniform blew his whistle and stopped traffic while the Mercedes driver got back in his vehicle and sped off into the night.

Two motorcycles and a police pick-up truck arrived. The motorcycles had black boxes on their back racks, and the long-haired young Chinese riders extracted large-format cameras and proceeded to document the travesty.

"Bloodsuckers," Boonsong said as he now opened the door for Martin to exit. "They take these photographs for a half dozen or so newspapers who'll splash their front page with full-color, blood-spattered images."

Martin knew this. He read at least two Thai papers every day, and was still amazed and mortified by their fascination with death and dismemberment in all its gory detail.

Boonsong continued: "They then post the best of their pictures outside the Chinese Benevolent Society, and tomorrow morning crowds will gather as they admire their collective good fortune at *not* being the ones in the photos."

The powerful flashes of the cameras added to the evolving light show. Thamarat cleared the way for two other cops who placed a rubber sheet over the body without so much as even checking for a pulse. They hoisted him into the rear of the pick-up along with his shattered bike.

Within ten minutes of their arrival they were gone, and a water truck washed the blood and human matter into the sewer.

Sergeant Thamarat was back at the wheel.

"That's it?" Martin asked as they pulled back into traffic.

"Yes," Boonsong replied. "Deputy Minister of Communications

Prinsat made a legal entry onto Silom Road after attending a state function at the Dusit Thani. The unfortunate motorcycle rider made an illegal collision with Khun Prinsat's vehicle."

"He looked drunk."

"No, Mr. Larue. You're mistaken. Khun Prinsat hadn't had anything to drink the entire evening."

"Yeah, right. And I'm the tooth fairy."

"I repeat. That's it. No need for an investigation. Case closed." Boonsong stared icily at Martin in the rear-view mirror, and Martin sank into his seat.

The rest of the night proved fairly slow after the gory entrée. Around midnight a tourist challenged an Indian tailor over the quality of a suit he'd already paid a hefty price for. He attacked the shopkeeper with his own shears, and was being restrained by two burly Sikhs just as Martin and company arrived.

Caucasian mannequins with pearl-white skin, orange razor-haircuts, wearing knock-offs of Armani and Hugo Boss filled the window of Dhaval's Tailor shop. Martin was actually impressed with the diplomatic manner in which Lieutenant-Colonel Boonsong defused the situation. He ordered the German tourist released and asked him to model the offending garment. Upon display, it was quite obvious the visitor had a legitimate complaint. The jacket and trousers appeared to be for two different people. While the German was fairly slim and evenly proportioned, the jacket was of enormous girth and resembled the giant suit worn by avant-garde musician David Byrne in the Talking Heads concert film *Stop Making Sense*. The pants were another matter altogether. Try as he might, he could not button them.

Dhaval had a string of excuses: Gunther had obviously lost a lot of weight, in defense of the jacket; but only in the upper torso, in defense of the pants.

"If it doesn't fit, you must acquit." Boonsong wisely suggested that Dhaval re-cut the jacket and re-make the pants, and after much protestation, the tailor agreed.

Martin thought that he might have his human interest story after all—the wise, benevolent police officer patrolling his beat with a sense of compassion and fairness—when Boonsong pocketed a 2,000-baht "fine" from Gunther for "threatening an act of violence."

Back in the car, Boonsong explained: "He can't expect to act violently and get away with it. In your country, I would have taken him to jail."

Martin mulled the logic of the last statement as they descended into the wee hours of the night.

———

As dawn approached, Martin was snoring soundly in the back of the Corolla. Boonsong and Thamarat were chatting idly, when the radio sparked to life. Thamarat responded, "Alpha Unit reads you. What's up?"

There was a moment of shrill static and then: "Another deposit has been made at Hernando Church."

Boonsong sat bolt upright and took the handset from Thamarat. "Boonsong here." He glanced at the rear. Martin was beginning to stir. "We're not in close proximity." There was an uncomfortable tone to his voice. "Can't Bravo Unit handle it?"

After more static, the radio replied, "Negative, sir. Bravo and Charlie units are on diplomatic escort to Don Muang." Martin was now wide-awake. "What's up?"

Boonsong ignored him. He thought a moment and then spoke into the handset: "All right HQ. Alpha Unit is en route."

The electronic lock on Martin's door suddenly clicked open. "Get out, Mr. Larue," Boonsong said to the rear-view mirror.

"Get out? You must be joking." Martin looked out at the deserted back street where they were parked, and shuddered. Rats the size of bulldogs scurried through the garbage scattered around the *soi*.

"It's four a.m., Colonel. Departing your company at this time and location could put me in great physical danger. I'm certain that the contract provided by Khun Prakasan assured my safe passage."

"To the contrary, Mr. Larue. Khun Prakasan signed a release of all liability…should anything happen to you tonight. You cannot expect 'safe passage' when you accompany a police patrol in Bangkok."

Released them from liability? Son of a bitch. Martin would deal with the little toad when this night was over.

"Colonel Boonsong. Be reasonable. I came along to get a story. If I leave now, I have nothing at all. I might even be forced to write a…" He swallowed to clear his dry throat. "A negative piece…depicting police favoritism to the elite, and bribery in the name of restitution."

Martin suddenly realized the possible consequences of what he'd just said, and he closed his eyes while he waited for Boonsong to draw his revolver.

Boonsong fixed him hard with his black eyes. "Very well, Mr. Larue. You should see your journey through to its end."

The lock slammed shut on Martin's door.

———

Hernando Church was the euphemism for a large marble mausoleum that stood in the center of a century-old cemetery. An entire city block of old burial sites and tombs, smack in the middle of Bangkok's financial district. Not in active use for over ten years, it presently belonged to the Assumption Church. The relocation of its occupants had been broached over a half dozen times in the last century, but each time the bureaucratic quagmire that such a mission would require, had caused its early abortion. It currently sat—an incongruous testament to a bygone age—surrounded by high-rise office buildings and abutting the Chong Nonsi skytrain station on the almost unpronounceable Narathivat-Rajanakarin Road.

The cemetery was divided into three sections. The first two, including the Hernando Mausoleum, accommodated mainly Thai and foreign residents: Spanish, Portuguese, French, Dutch, and the occasional American. These were mainly in above-ground tombs— a tribute to Bangkok's notorious flooding during the rainy season. Scattered around the wildly overgrown ground were hundreds of rag-tag crosses.

The third section was Thai-Chinese. In contrast to the others, these graves were well maintained, with bright fuchsias climbing the vines of an old arbor at the entrance. Photos of the deceased adorned most of the tombs.

A familiar-looking police pick-up truck was parked parallel to the open gate. Unlike at the accident scene earlier, its lights were off, and the cemetery was in relative darkness, save for the glow of the full moon.

As before, Boonsong and Thamarat exited the vehicle and left Martin locked in the rear. They approached a junior officer who snap-saluted them and then led them through the gate.

Screw this. Martin reached through the open divider Sergeant Thamarat had neglected to close, and pressed the rear door lock button on the center console that ran between the front seats. A free man, he stepped out of the car, then cautiously into the moonlit cemetery.

Boonsong and Thamarat were engaged in a quiet discussion at the entrance to the mausoleum. An ornamental iron gate was open behind them, and the uniformed officer's flashlight beam played into the dusty corners.

Thamarat motioned to Boonsong, who turned and confronted

Martin. "You should have stayed in the car," he growled.

"What's going on here?" Martin stepped forward and Sergeant Thamarat made a move to stop him. But he was too late.

Martin stood frozen at the spectacle within.

"My God."

A girl with dyed hair was sprawled naked across the cold stone bier in the center of the tomb. She was no more than twenty years old; her head was tilted back, and her upside-down eyes stared lifelessly at Martin. Her expression was one of pure ecstasy, as if death had provided her the greatest pleasure of her short life. Her mouth was wide-open and curled into a smile. She was laid out, spread-eagled, displayed as a macabre joke.

Martin was drawn to her. As he moved around her, he couldn't help but notice the dried blood that had seeped from her finely haired vagina and ran down her inner thighs. Her clothing was ripped to shreds and lay scattered about the floor.

Boonsong gently closed the girl's eyes.

"Who is she?" Martin reached out for the wall and steadied himself.

"Who knows? A child of the street. A homeless victim of Bangkok's economic woes."

Martin frowned. "The market crash seems to have hit her a lot harder than most people I know. Seriously, what happened here?"

"That is difficult to say, Mr. Larue. Now, please step back while Officer Rangchit removes the corpse."

"What! Remove the corpse…? What about an investigation? What about evidence? DNA?"

Boonsong sighed. He motioned to Sergeant Thamarat. "Restrain Mr. Larue and take him back to the car. Drive him to his apartment. If he offers any further resistance, shoot him."

Sergeant Thamarat moved toward Martin.

"What the fuck? Keep your hands off me, Sergeant… This is ridiculous. I want to know who the girl is…and why she was murdered."

"You're assuming that her death was neither accidental or self-inflicted, Mr. Larue. Your assumptions are dangerous and you're interfering with a police investigation."

"I'm *assuming* she didn't rip off her clothes, climb atop a tomb, and slash her pussy, yes. I'm *assuming* she didn't kill herself. And you're about to throw her in a bag and dispose of her. Why?"

"Now Sergeant!" Boonsong barked.

Thamarat pulled Martin's hands behind his back and clamped on a pair of handcuffs before he could resist. He shoved Martin, who slipped on the blood that had congealed on the marble floor. He fell and banged his head on the corner of the tomb.

He saw stars.

4

———————

Sunlight…

It burned through the teakwood slats and inched its way across the granite floor. Within minutes it would reach the slumbering figure, rendering the most intolerable damage.

Closer and closer the shafts of light crept up the silken sheets. Moving sensuously over their victim, they soon made first contact with bare flesh.

"Aaagghh."

Martin pulled the sheets over his head, which throbbed as he tried to reconstruct the night. He didn't recall drinking anything. As a rule he didn't imbibe—mainly due to consequences such as he was experiencing now. He felt his head gently, and winced at the golfball-sized lump on his frontal lobe.

That bastard Boonsong. Now he remembered everything… everything that is except arriving back at his apartment on Soi Lang Suan.

"Daeng," he called, and his girlfriend soon appeared. She was in her mid-twenties, tall and willowy, and bore the detached air that comes naturally to a beauty being ignored.

"How did I get here last night?"

"I suppose you walked. How should I know? You rang the bell at four-thirty and woke me from a beautiful dream. I found you passed out in the lobby. You're really a terrible drunk."

"I didn't drink anything. Look at this." He pointed out the red lump.

"So you get drunk and fall down. Serves you right."

"I didn't get drunk! I was with the police. Would you please get me some ice and some aspirin?"

She sighed and shuffled out of the room.

Women. Martin frowned. Sometimes he thought of Daeng as a necessary evil. She kept his books, arranged his travel, virtually arranged his life. Without her, he admitted, even with all his wealth, he'd be lost. But God she could be a pain in the ass. If he didn't love her so much…

He refused to finish that thought, and concentrated instead on the night just passed…much as he could bear to think through the throbbing pain.

Lieutenant-Colonel Boonsong had threatened him, that was quite clear. Yet, what wasn't clear was *why*? Why did he not want Martin to see him conduct his investigation into the girl's death? Why was the corpse being removed so quickly? What was going on?

Daeng appeared with a bucket of ice, a towel, a glass of water, and a bottle of aspirin. All neatly arranged on a laminated tray.

He thanked her and downed three of the aspirins.

He grabbed a handful of ice, wrapped it in the towel, and placed it on his swollen head.

"Ahhhh. Now close the blinds will you please, Daeng?" He lay back on the bed while she did as he asked. He was feeling the first signs of relief as she left the room.

"Drunken fool," she said as she shut the door.

Ain't love grand? Martin wrapped the sheets around him.

———

A week passed and Martin allowed his temper to cool to a reasonable simmer. As arrogant as he was, he knew better than to storm off and challenge the integrity of a commanding police officer. Such things got people killed, especially *farangs*. So he waited.

He waited, and he read. Four Thai and two English-language papers each day.

Nothing.

Three days went by and not a word in print about the poor girl found dead in a city graveyard that hadn't been used in ten years. He avoided the daily calls from Managing Editor Prakasan, and was ready to forget the whole thing when Daeng handed him the latest copy of *Thai Rath*.

He leafed through it quickly, as Daeng was eager to wrap some fish heads in it to take to her brother. There, on the second to last page, he saw her. In a grainy blow-up from a New Years Eve party at the Patpong bar where she was last employed, the girl stared at him again. This time, however, her eyes were full of life. Her hair was darker than when he saw her on her deathbed, but it was unmistakably the same girl. He read the headline attached to the short article: GIRL DROWNS IN CHAO PHRAYA.

Martin couldn't believe his eyes. He read on:

Police in the Bangrak district were called to Si Phraya pier last night to recover the body of 19-year-old Kimara "Kimchi" Sittharotsak. The girl was employed as a barmaid at Goldfingers Bar on Soi Patpong, and owner Randall Tinsley said she was reliable and dependable and he had been concerned when she failed to show for work for three days.

Police Sergeant Thamarat Suksomboon said the body had been spotted by two "night fishermen" who immediately called the authorities. Foul play has been ruled out, and her death listed as accidental drowning. "She probably slipped and fell off the pier while waiting for a ferry," Sergeant Thamarat said, noting that the girl resided on the Thonburi side of the river and regularly took the ferry home. Her family has been notified, and her body will be cremated in Bangkok, according to their wishes."

"Daeng, this is the girl." He showed her the picture and the article. "That's the same girl I saw spread-eagled, naked and dead in Hernando Cemetery."

"Says here she drowned."

"I know that's what it says. That's what the police want you to believe."

"Why should they care what *I believe*? I believe the newspaper. They don't lie. You…you lie all the time."

"Daeng, they're lying for a reason. *What* reason I don't know."

———

And so Martin took the skytrain once again to Mor Chit, and a cab to the *Times*.

Managing Editor Prakasan met him at the door to his office. "Ahh, Martin. Delighted to see you. I've been waiting breathlessly for a full report on your night patrol. It must have been fraught with danger and excitement. Tell me all."

"It was as exciting as I care for my nights to be. As for *danger*, that may lay ahead."

Martin sat in the rosewood chair

"Intriguing. Please, from the top."

Martin described the night's events, starting with corpse number one, the unfortunate motorcycle rider who crossed the path of a powerful and possibly inebriated politician, and concluding with dead body number two, the naked girl stretched out on a tombstone. When he finished, he opened the *Thai Rath* and pointed to the smiling teenager. "That's her."

"Extraordinary. Why are they covering up her murder?"

"I have no idea."

Prakasan was delighted with the intrigue. "I *knew* you

would come up with a story. But this…corruption and deception by the commanding officer…it's just what we need."

Martin couldn't believe what he was hearing. "Now hold on a minute. I'm not writing any story of police corruption."

"Oh, but you must, Martin. I've been trying to catch Lieutenant-Colonel Boonsong with his hand in the cookie jar for ten years. But nothing ever pans out. But you, in one evening, you expose him for the crook I've always suspected him to be. Oh, this is delicious."

"This is not *delicious*, this is scary." He tapped on the *Thai Rath* article for emphasis. "I don't know what's going on here."

"Then you must find out. Investigate."

"*Investigate*? Look, I don't know who you think I am, but Philip Marlowe I'm not."

"You are a writer, Martin. A fine writer who can accomplish far more than pleasant summations of the worthless plagiarism that's insultingly referred to as *cinema* these days."

"Don't patronize me, Khun Prakasan. I was even handcuffed and bludgeoned—*a little exaggeration*—by these two 'policemen'…because I saw something they didn't want me to see. I enjoy life, Khun Prakasan, and I intend to keep on enjoying it." He headed for the door. "Get one of your staff writers to *investigate* it."

"None of my Thai writers would touch it, Martin. It's your story. You get me facts that we can prove, and the *Times* will protect you."

"*Protect me*?" Martin laughed. "This is Bangkok. Life is cheap. And I'm a *farang*…a rich *farang*, mind you. I imagine I'm worth at least 500 dollars. That's about the going rate for assassinations these days."

Prakasan smiled at him as he went out the door. "Martin. I have a suggestion for you."

This stopped him. "What?"

"Start with the cemetery."

5

Eighty-year-old Usa "Yudie" Samsarat heard something crack as she slowly straightened up. She was certain it was her back, finally giving out. It wasn't of course, as she was now standing upright. Well…fairly upright. Forty-five years of pulling weeds and picking up wind-blown trash had left her with the posture of a toad, and she relied heavily on a strong bamboo cane. She had stepped on a broken beer bottle, one of dozens left by the street vendors who paid a pittance to store their carts behind the gates and then proceeded to use the graveyard as their own personal *pissoir*. How she loathed them. She carried a spray bottle of lye mixed with alcohol to scrub the yellow stains off the old graves that she was paid to maintain.

Those names not on the tattered old list given her by the great-grandson of Juan Hernando were left alone. Occasionally a relative or friend came in and scraped away years of accumulated grime, and straightened the ornate crosses on those interred in the ground. They would leave fresh flowers, and offerings of fruit and whiskey. Within hours, the lousy *soi* vendors would eat the fruit, drink the whiskey, and piss on the grave. Oh that one of *them* should fall under her care. That grave would become a garbage bin, repaying its occupant's total disregard for those who slept beneath his feet. As it was, Yudie's main responsibility were the tombs that rested above the ground.

HERMANN MONTREAUX, B. 1844 TUSCANY, D. 1904 AYUTTHAYA

Signor Montreaux's white-bearded countenance stared out from the daguerreotype, as he had done for 98 years. As Yudie whisked her broom across the old man, he spoke to her: "*Kor tort khrap. Khun Yai, chuay phom dai mai?*"

"Aaaiii! *Phii*! I knew one day it would happen." Yudie threw herself to her knees and began *waiing*, her palms pressed tightly together to her forehead, fingers pointed to the heavens.

"Madam?" The ghost spoke once more, only now his voice was behind her.

Peering through her clasped hands, she cautiously turned her head.

"Grandmother, can you help me please?" Martin repeated. He wore his customary light silk shirt rolled at the sleeves, and a soft Panama hat. He took a handkerchief from his pocket and mopped his sweaty brow.

"Oiiii? What does a white devil want in my garden?" Yudie always referred to the cemetery as her "garden."

"It's a beautiful garden, and you tend to it with the loving care a mother gives to a daughter." Martin sweet-talked the lie with precise inflection and without a trace of accent.

"*Farang*. You speak good Thai. Help me up please. I am very old." Yudie put out her arthritis-riddled hand, and Martin gently helped the old lady to her feet. "Don't scare me again. Next time I fear I won't be able to rise. Hand me my cane please."

Martin retrieved her walking stick and she sat down on Signor Montreaux's tomb. "Now, what is it you want, young man?"

Flattery. My God, the old crone is flirting with me. He sat next to her, the marble feeling deliciously cool through his thin linen slacks.

"Grandmother, I'd like to ask you some questions, regarding your 'garden.' I'm quite prepared to pay for the answers." Martin opened his wallet and extracted two 1,000-baht notes.

"Ahhh, my favorite picture of His Majesty. For bringing me such lovely gifts, I invite you to my home, where we can talk in the shade." Yudie rose to her full semi-erect stature and, leaning on her stick, she waddled up the gravel path between the tombs.

Her house was inside the perimeter of the cemetery, nestled up against a high whitewashed wall which effectively separated her from the world of the living—and the twenty-first century for that matter. A clapboard construction with a tin roof, it was little more than a squatter's shack, but Yudie kept it neat and clean, and the same fuchsia-colored flowers she planted in the graveyard twined around the posts of her porch. She and Martin sat on her modest veranda sipping cold tea and facing the cemetery.

"How long have you tended the cemetery?" Martin asked.

"Almost half a century. Used to be busy job, but we've had no new guests for ten years now."

Martin admired the view. Not exactly the kind of vista that would elevate property values. "You've lived here all that time?"

"Yes, yes. But I nearly had a modern house. At Bang Bua Thong. Husband and I won the lottery and made a deposit on a retirement home in a beautiful modern village. Three Lakes." She held up three of her withered fingers for emphasis. "Two bedrooms, air-con, tile floor, picture window…*suay maak*."

Martin got the picture. In Thailand's boom of the eighties and early nineties, hideous Romanesque housing developments sprang up all over the kingdom. Designed without a hint of planning for their tropical climate, they were full of the features the nouveaux riches associated with their wealth, picture windows being one of them. Never mind that the huge panes of unventilated glass forced the interior temperatures into the triple digits; this was the future— and the lovely drawings of how it would all be wonderfully landscaped and groomed, found Thais and a few hapless foreigners shelling out Beverly Hills prices for cement and stucco boxes that sat side by side in dusty lots, stripped of all vegetation and never completed.

"Husband was no good. Gambled and drank whiskey. Spent all the money we won. I kept thinking, when do I get to retire? When do I get to take a break? I have a son. Jadesada. But he was born crippled and I was forced to sell him to the arbiter who runs the mob. He's begged all his life on a Sukhumvit bridge."

She shook her head at the memory. "My poor, poor boy. Lord Buddha how I miss him." She wiped a tear and continued: "By the time I reached 65, my husband dropped dead. Heart attack in a whorehouse." She spat and muttered a totally untranslatable Thai curse.

"I found out he borrowed from the bank again and again. Now, instead of a nice little home, all paid off, I have nothing. So I have no choice. I live in my garden, talk to no one. Just waiting for my day to be planted here." She sighed, as deep and resonant a sound as Martin could recall.

He was touched by this old woman and wanted to take her into his arms. He knew that she'd been alone for years and years. He saw it in her sweet smile and he imagined her as a young girl. He could picture her playing in the *klongs*, innocent of the life of pain, hardship, and loneliness that awaited her. He held back a tear, an emotion that for him was quite unusual.

"Grandmother, you see all that goes on here, don't you?" Martin asked.

"I see what I want." Her mouth formed a frown. "There's such that goes on late at night that I want no part of."

"Such as?"

"Sinners. Those unwashed scum that store their carts in here." She pointed toward a half dozen wheeled stalls that were lined up haphazardly at the entrance. "They have a key to the gate. They return late at night and desecrate the hallowed ground with their drinking and fornicating."

Martin probed further. "They ever take their 'sinning' into the Hernando family tomb?" He looked at the grand, domed edifice that dominated the graveyard. A chill went through him as the image of the ravaged girl came back to him. He shuddered and shook it off.

"No. That is locked. Only the family have the key." Yudie looked away and seemed distant.

"It was open last Friday night," Martin boldly offered. "I was here. The police were here."

She looked back at him. "If the police were here, they'd have the key, wouldn't they?"

"I don't know. Do they?"

"They have. I saw Diego Hernando give the key to them the first time—"

"The 'first time?' The first time what, Grandmother?"

"Nothing… I didn't say anything." She rose from her chair, unsteady until she clutched her cane.

"The first time a young girl's body was found there…? Is that right, Grandmother?"

She was waddling toward her door. Her gait was shaky and she seemed pale.

"How many have there been, Grandmother? When did it start?" He was almost shouting now.

She was at the door. She spoke, but did not look back at him. "We are finished, Mister."

Desperate, Martin tried one last ploy. "When was it that Diego
Hernando gave the key to the police?"

"Ten years ago."

Inside, she shut her door on Martin Larue and the rest of the world.

———

Martin spent the next two days going through the *Bangkok Times'* archives. The previous two years were easy. They were all stored and retrieved electronically. Data was simply cross-referenced and downloaded. But anything prior to 1999 took a trip to the *real* archives.

It was row upon row of bundled clippings. The archivist, Penny, was very kind in the assistance she offered as Martin made his way through the files—fortunately sorted into broad categories—but he came away with a headache, frustrated and feeling that he was missing something. He had searched for any mention of Hernando Cemetery, but all he found were a few obituaries from 1992. The details of the internments were morbidly fascinating but of no use to him. No murders, no naked girls dead or alive. He *had* found a significant number of other dead girls, however. Bangkok seemed to inspire young women to take their lives: jumping into *klongs*, off buildings, walking in front of speeding lorries, almost a weekly occurrence —but only after November 1992. *Ten years ago.*

The next day he spent repeating the same search at *Thai Rath*. Oddly enough, though they had computerized their files about the same time as the *Times*, they had scanned their back issues to 1995. It didn't take long to realize that he was getting virtually the same information, and after searching their items for 1992, he gave up.

As he exited the building, his head throbbing, he was almost hit by a motorcycle. He stepped back onto the curb as the rider gave him the finger. Some things were universal. As he watched him heading away, long black hair flying in the wind, he remembered something. Something that he had found bizarre on that night that now seemed so long ago.

The Chinese Benevolent Society. If what Lieutenant-Colonel Boonsong had told him was true, now *there* was an archive worth investigating.

———

Exiting the taxi at the corner of Yaowarat and Yaowapanit roads in the heart of Chinatown, Martin walked parallel to the Talad Kao market. Soon he came upon a small crowd gathered in front of an old Chinese building. Smoking clay pipes and stroking thin, gray beards, a half dozen old men studied two glass cases that contained black and white photos. Moving closer, Martin could see the blood and dismemberment that were the main feature of each.

There was a buzzer next to the shuttered, heavy double doors. A typed note, in Cantonese and worn yellow with age, identified the occupant as Master Teng Wu. Martin pushed the buzzer and waited.

A minute passed and nothing happened as he was subjected to quizzical stares by the elderly Chinese. He smiled and nodded and rang the buzzer again. A small, wrinkled man took his intricately carved walking stick and rapped loudly on the door. Immediately there was a response from inside.

"*Wei?*" The door opened a crack and a pair of spectacled eyes peered out.

"Master Teng?" Martin queried.

"Yes." Master Teng opened the door, and Martin extended his card with the title *JOURNALIST* translated into Thai, Japanese, and Chinese. Below were his various contact numbers.

Seemingly impressed, Master Teng guided Martin into the dimly lit interior.

Master Teng took a seat behind a gray metal desk covered in piles of papers and files. He lit a cigarette and laid the match in the huge glass ashtray that was full of butts. It was obvious that Master Teng did not employ the services of a maid.

"What can I do for you…Mr. Larue?"

"I'm wondering if you keep an archive of your material."

"My 'material'?" Master Teng looked puzzled.

"The photos that you display outside."

Martin tried to get comfortable in an ancient armchair, but

the stuffing was mostly gone, and springs were poking through the seat cushion.

"Ahh, the photos. If you noticed, Mr. Larue, the photos fill just two small cases. The rest of the building's facade, almost an entire block, is dedicated to a bulletin board with hundreds of postings available to the Chinese community. There are doctors and clinics offering vaccinations, breast examinations, rectal exams…all matters pertaining to a healthy life are listed. There are notices of agricultural interest for those whose economic fate is tied to the rice fields of the motherland. You'll see that religious services and all manner of secular matters dominate almost half the space. Local obituaries, astrological forecasts, numerical castings, and mahjong postings fill the remainder. So you can see that the depictions of the unfortunate are but a small part of the community service we provide."

"It's the photographs that interest me, Master Teng. When did the practice of displaying the pictures of the 'unfortunates' begin?" Martin had to stand. He looked for another empty chair, but all were reserved for paperwork.

"It was 1972…the Year of the Rat. I know because it was the second year of my arrival in Bangkok. At that time there was only one Chinese-language newspaper. Master Chen, my predecessor, would buy two copies and carefully tack up the pages, displaying the entire newspaper. He soon found that the pages with photos of accidents and other misfortunes went missing within hours, and that the rest of the paper was ignored. So he installed the two locked glass cases, made an arrangement with a number of photographers to make copies of their prints—published and unpublished—and those became what he displayed on that gruesome subject. It has brought, I am sorry to say, some notoriety to our mission. I am not entirely in favor of the policy. But it has become such a popular attraction that I'm afraid to discontinue it. And it brings no end of gifts and donations from benefactors who count their daily blessings…by viewing those less fortunate."

Martin hesitated before asking, "Are the photos archived?"

"Oh heaven's, yes. But by date alone, I'm afraid." Master Teng snubbed out his cigarette.

"Might I have a look at them? I'd be glad to make a donation."

"A donation would be much appreciated, Mr. Larue. But I'm afraid that to go through the entire catalogue would be quite exhausting. Is there a specific date we can start with?"

There was, and Martin soon found himself in a moldy concrete room with a large stainless-steel table and hundreds of dark-green file boxes. Each had a hand-printed date on a yellowed file card attached to its front. He began with the summer of 1992.

The horror of each stark image was hard for Martin to stomach. These were far more graphic than anything he'd seen at either the *Times* or *Thai Rath*. Most would be rejected by the Western press, and hardly any had been published even in Thailand where gory magazines like *191*—named after the police emergency number—were big sellers.

After an hour, he had to take a break. He walked out into the street to clear his head.

He re-entered the archive and plunged back in. Within ten minutes he came across an image that almost caused his heart to stop. He flipped the eight-by-ten, and read the date on the back: November 25th, 1992.

He slowly turned it back, afraid that the image would have changed, but there it was: a young girl, naked, eyes open to the camera, spread-eagled atop the tomb in Hernando's mausoleum.

Inside the file there were five more photographs of the same subject. Except for the physical difference of this victim compared to Kimchi—long, jet-black hair; high cheekbones;

darker skin; and taller—the crime scene was identical to the one he had witnessed only days before.

Martin was trembling with excitement. There was an ancient Xerox machine in the corner, and he hastily copied the pictures.

He spent the rest of the afternoon pouring through another ten years of horrors, finding photos of three more girls splayed out atop Hernando's tomb: March 1993, September 1996, and October 1997.

All the shots, including those from 1992, bore the same rubber stamp on the back: NO REPRODUCTION WITHOUT CREDIT. WASIT NING ZUO. Below each was a phone number, which was different in each case. The photo for '97 had a mobile number. Martin wrote down all four numbers.

6

"Ning" as he was known, was already seated at the trendy Italian restaurant on Soi Saladaeng. He was well into a fifty-dollar bottle of Merlot as Martin arrived.

Bangkok was full of trendy Italian restaurants catering to the Thai yuppies' new-found taste for robust reds and pasta. For Martin, who was on a permanent diet, the trend was slightly annoying in that his social calendar usually included a half dozen dinners each week he was in town—and more than half of those, by default, were held in upmarket Italian bistros. Each one meant another lost week in the battle of the bulge. He sighed and ordered a calamari salad and *nam* soda.

"So, Martin, what can I do for you?" Ning finally asked as he poured himself more of the Merlot.

Cheeky bastard. Martin calculated that whatever information he gleaned from Ning would set him back at least 200 dollars for the dinner alone. He opened the envelope and laid out the Xeroxes of Ning's photos.

"Ahh. I remember these." Ning smiled as he picked up one of the grizzly images. "The graveyard series. Are you a collector?"

"Not exactly, but I am interested in these particular shots, though you just might have others that would interest me."

A plate of thinly sliced prosciutto and melon arrived, along with some lovely sliced tomato and mozzarella garnished with a light olive oil. The waiter ground a typically miniscule amount of black pepper over each dish from an appropriately massive pepper mill.

Ning dug in while Martin watched. Between mouthfuls of antipasto, the photographer studied the copies of his own work. "What do you want to know?"

Martin put the first picture, the one from November '92, on the top of the pile. "Do you remember shooting this?"

"Of course. Quite good don't you think? I was very disappointed when no one printed it."

"Why was that?"

"I don't know. The story never appeared." He flipped through the other photos. "None of these were ever published."

"Colonel Boonsong?" Martin offered.

"Boonsong?" Ning laughed. "You know the honorable officer?"

Martin nodded.

"Then we shouldn't have to discuss him." He polished off the tomato and mozzarella. "Some things are better left unsaid. I don't know about you, but I have to work for a living." He filled his glass with the last of the Merlot and ordered another bottle.

Martin re-calculated. *Two hundred and fifty dollars.* He went back to the first photo. "Tell me what happened this night."

"I heard the call on my CB radio. Another dead body. They didn't identify the location, just gave an address near Silom Road. I was quite surprised to find it was Hernando Cemetery."

Ning's medallions of veal with a side of pasta arrived. "The girl was very pale. She appeared virtually drained of blood, but there wasn't that much pooled up on the floor. I've seen a lot of dead bodies, hundreds in fact, and when there's been a laceration, the amount of blood is unreal." He started in on the pasta. "But there *was* a laceration in this case?"

"Where was it?"

"I couldn't tell for sure. But there was a lot of blood on her legs." He paused, remembering. "It was spooky. I shot my photos and got the hell out."

"And this one?" Martin pointed at the picture from March '93.

"Same thing." He drained his glass while the waiter opened the new bottle. "I can save a lot of time here. On each occasion, I heard the call on my radio. I get to the cemetery and there's another girl dead. I shoot my photos, get the hell out of there, and each time the pictures never get printed. Nothing changed, except..." he flipped through the pictures, "...for this time."

In the photo from October '97, Lieutenant-Colonel Boonsong was captured. Five years seemed to make little difference. He was the same old Boonsong, his scowl expressing his displeasure.

Why didn't I notice this before?

"You see, I ride a Kawasaki 750. I usually get to the scene long before the cops. Get in and get out. Each time, I arrived before there were any officers on the scene. Just a brainless helmet cop. I give him fifty baht, shoot my pictures, and get the fuck out of there. But this time, Boonsong arrived while I was shooting." He shook his head. "Boonsong *had a cow.* You know that expression?"

Martin nodded. He'd seen "The Simpsons."

"Started screaming, demanded my film."

Martin looked again at the picture. "What did you do?"

Ning smiled as he chewed rapidly. "Old trick. Opened the wrong camera and gave him a blank roll. He ripped it open and threw the useless film into a pool of blood. He drew his pistol and I backed out the fucking door, *waiing* like a peasant all the way."

He took a last forkful of veal and wiped his greasy lips. "That was the last time I went to Hernando Cemetery."

"Did you ever hear it mentioned on the radio again?"

"Occasionally." Ning called for the dessert menu. "Actually, I heard a call to the cemetery, just last week."

Martin winced with the painful reminder. "But you didn't go?"

"Fuck no."

"I did." Martin showed Ning the *Thai Rath* article with Kimchi's picture. "I was on a ride-along with the Bangrak police. We went to Hernando Cemetery that night. This girl was stretched across the slab. Her hair was dyed blonde, but it was this girl."

Ning expressed mild interest, but was sidetracked by the arrival of his tiramisu and espresso. He sipped his coffee and asked the waiter for a brandy.

"Ning. Read the article. It says she drowned in the Chao Phraya."

He scanned the piece. "I'm not surprised. It always seemed to me the police were covering something up."

"Like a serial killer?"

"Could be." Ning shrugged.

The Hennessy arrived and he downed it in one gulp.

"Did you ever say anything to anyone?"

"Like who? The police?" Ning laughed and pushed his chair away from the table. "It's really none of my business, Martin. I thank you for the dinner." He stood, burped, and was gone.

Martin looked mournfully at the nearly full second bottle of Merlot, then the waiter brought the bill: 350 US dollars.

The next day, Martin returned to the offices of *Thai Rath* and researched the dates of the four cemetery photos. By going through the successive issues of the paper after each date in question, he found, in every case, a dead girl whose description or photo was exactly the same as the victim in each cemetery shot:

Tessarawat Poonyang. Aged 21. Recently arrived from Laos. No apparent source of income. Fell or leapt to her death from the nineteenth floor of the Tower Inn Hotel on Silom Road. Conveniently located next to the Hernando Cemetery, Martin noted.

Wat Thankasarin, 19, from Surin. A waitress at the Superstar Bar on Patpong 1, found with her throat slit and left in a dumpster behind Foodland. This story had a photo, and she was almost a perfect match to girl number two.

Pacharee "Pookie" Noonsatary, 17, Bangkok-born. A student at St. John's—socially and economically a cut above the others — drowned in a *klong* north of the Hilton Hotel. Again, there was a picture, and again she was undeniably the girl in the graveyard shot.

Last there was Witsara "Nit Noi" Kinbarra, 22. A mother of two, no known income, divorced, recently arrived from Udon Thani. Nit Noi also leapt to her death from the Tower Inn. No photo, but to Martin there was no doubt. There was a serial murderer hard at work in Bangkok, and the Bangrak police were covering his tracks.

Armed with this information, Martin returned to the office of Managing Editor Prakasan.

———

"Well done, Mr. Larue. Well done indeed," Prakasan crowed. "This is marvelous."

Ning's photos of crime scenes and related newspaper clippings were spread out across the managing editor's desk.

"This is hideous," Martin countered. "A serial killer allowed to prowl undetected for ten or more years? I've counted five victims, but who knows how many more he's destroyed?"

"Yes. Yes. Wonderful stuff. And the police are covering it up? Oh, it couldn't be better." Prakasan beamed.

"It couldn't be *worse*." Martin scowled.

"Martin, you must write this up. I will hold the front page on Sunday for you."

The front page! *Sunday*! *Jesus.* That was a long way from film reviews.

"I can't do it."

"Of course you can, dear boy. Just assemble the facts, the way you told me here." Prakasan was fascinated by the images. He kept picking them up and examining them. "Marvelous photos. You say this fellow Ning has all the negatives?"

"Yes." He took the photos from Prakasan. "Something has to be done about this. I thoroughly agree. But if I write this, it'll get me killed. *That* I'm sure of."

"Martin, let's be serious about this. If you want, we'll publish it anonymously. But I think that's a huge mistake."

"Look, you offered me protection. What does that mean?"

"Anything you need. Security guards, bodyguards...day and night. Whatever it takes to make you feel comfortable." Prakasan stood and walked around the desk. "Martin, your best protection is freedom of the press. It may not seem like it sometimes, but Thailand is a democracy, and our rights as journalists are protected. Boonsong knows this, and I'm sure he'd be very wary of crossing that line... I do have one suggestion, though."

"What's that?" Martin asked.

"I wouldn't mention him by name."

BANGRAK SERIAL KILLER read the 90-point boldface headline on Sunday's *Bangkok Times*.

> *The mutilated bodies of five young women between the ages of 17 and 22 are known to have been discovered in the Hernando Cemetery on Silom Road between November 25th, 1992 and last Friday. Rather than investigating these grizzly murders directly, the Bangrak police are suspected of being involved in a cover-up, going so far as to actually falsify the causes of death and location of the discovery of the girls' bodies.*

Martin awoke to the news being served to him with his breakfast.

As agreed, his by-line was omitted from the front page, but it was attached to the end of the 2,000-word article.

Martin's carefully worded and well-edited story didn't mention Lieutenant-Colonel Boonsong by name, but it did identify the five girls, and it certainly pointed an accusing finger in the direction of Bangkok's finest.

He decided that this would be a day perhaps best spent in bed.He turned off the phone and pulled up the sheets.

———

A week passed before he got his first real 'response.' Oh, there were calls. Lots of calls. Friends calling to see if it was really him. Wanting to know what possessed him to write such a thing. Friends congratulating him on having the balls to expose what all of them took to be common knowledge about the police—and wondering where he was moving to?

And of course there was the response from the police: "There is no cause for alarm. We're sure there's a logical explanation to all this, and we are conducting a thorough investigation into these accusations."

But the first real response came rather late at night. Martin had taken Prakasan at his word and had him assign a full-time, live-in bodyguard. Hans was the bulky German's name, and Martin rather enjoyed his company. He could go out where he chose, Hans always at his side. Daeng thought he was *weird*, but that was only to be expected. Martin took to his normal social rounds, Hans in tow.

But one evening, after Daeng left he and Hans at the apartment entrance while she went to park the car, he heard a very strange *gurgling* sound from Hans. When he turned, he found that Hans was minus his most distinguishing feature—his large German head.

Martin gagged and choked as Hans' headless corpse crumpled to the pavement.

"Oh my God!" Martin shrieked.

"*God* had nothing to do with it," the man said as he emerged from the shadows.

With the street lamp back-lighting his long hair, the intruder stepped forward and Martin gasped as he made out the stranger's features. He was tall, over six feet, well built, and European. He wore an unconstructed silk suit of a deep beige, and a light-tan, open-collared shirt. He appeared to be about 35, but there were streaks of gray in his tousled hair. His eyes

—Good God, his eyes!— had a yellow luminescence where there would normally be white, rather like the symptoms a malaria patient manifests. His pupils were dark-green and heavily dilated. Martin could only compare them to those of a cat. There was a sheen of sweat on the man's brow, with a distinct red tint to the perspiration. In one hand he held a serrated, bone-handled knife. In the other—*Oh Lord, please spare me!—*was Hans' severed head, eyes bulging and the mouth gaping open.

The intruder raised the head and drank the blood that ran from the severed veins.

Martin staggered back in shock. The man finished his gruesome cocktail, and with one swift motion flung the head into the street where it bounced and rolled like a soccer ball. Two scruffy *soi* dogs suddenly appeared, and one scooped it up and ran off with it, the other cur barking at his heels.

The man wiped his bloody mouth with the back of his hand. He licked the blade and closed the knife, slipping it into his pocket.

Martin realized that the intruder's gaze had remained solidly fixed on him. He tried to run, but his legs were like rubber and wouldn't move. He tried to cry out, but he couldn't get enough air to make a sound.

The man lifted the corpse and stuffed it into a rubbish bin in the side alley. He slammed the lid and returned to the apartment entry. Martin was frozen in place. There was a small pool of blood on the sepia-toned, glazed tile floor. The intruder tilted a decorative *klong* jar, and the collected rainwater washed the blood into the street. He righted the jar and turned to Martin. "It's so tiresome cleaning up." He moved forward.

Martin swore he never saw his feet move, but suddenly the man was no more than an inch from his face. He breathed in deep and sniffed, the way a dog or a wolf sniffs another, getting a scent and learning from it.

"W-what do you want?"

"What do I want...? *Everything.*" The man smiled. "I want it all." He put his arm around Martin and literally swept him off his feet and out into Sarasin Road…

Lumpini Park floated by as if in a dream. They swooped through the entry to Brown Sugar Café, up the spiral stairs, and settled into a dark corner booth.

On the small stage below, a jazz combo played a straight-ahead version of Cole Porter's classic "Ev'ry Time We Say Goodbye," a young Filipina perfectly emulating Chet Baker's interpretation of the lyrics. The music drifted up to the second-floor and intoxicated Martin. It seemed the most beautiful music he'd ever heard. The café, which he had frequented on numerous occasions, seemed fresh and new and *wonderful*. The faux Tiffany lights cast a warm glow, the soft hues of the fabrics adorning the tables blending with the collage of posters on the walls. The food aromas mingled with the perfume and colognes…*totally and utterly intoxicating*. It was a sensuous den of earthly delights and Martin reveled in it.

A beautiful waitress appeared, and he fell instantly, madly in love with her. The man ordered a bottle of Chateau Haut-Brion and sent her away before Martin could protest.

"Beautiful, yes?" He asked with a smile.

"Gorgeous," Martin allowed. "I must have her."

"And so must I… Later. But first, I have a few questions for you, and I assume you have a few of your own."

Martin didn't reply. He was absorbed in the music, the light, the aromas…and the vision of the departing waitress. He was enraptured.

God. Why have I never noticed how wonderful this place was before?

The thought flitted by.

"Ramonne Delacroix. That is my name."

"Martin Larue." He had to recall his own name and it took a few moments to say it.

"I know, Mr. Larue. I sought *you* out, remember?" Ramonne was becoming annoyed at Martin's somnambulant manner. He quickly passed a hand in front of Martin's eyes and it was like the falling of a veil. The room was now somber in tone and color. The music subsided and the aromas dissipated.

"My God, who are you?" Martin shrank back in horror as reality returned.

"You keep calling to God, Mr. Larue, and I have to question His direct involvement here. He may have had a hand in my creation, as He no doubt has in the creation of *all* His creatures. But the true moment of my transformation into the *creature* who sits before you now, *that* act of transgression was, I fear, done in God's absence. Had *He* indeed been present, I doubt that He'd have allowed it, as my very presence here defies all laws of God and man."

The waitress arrived with the wine. Martin tried to speak to her, to warn her, to cry out for help, but he was unable to utter a single sound. Unable to move, he sat silently and watched Ramonne flirt with her as she uncorked the vintage Bordeaux. He brushed his fingers lightly across her hand as she poured the bottle, and she swooned.

"Anything else, please?" She asked nervously.

"Nothing for now, *mon cherie*." Ramonne smiled and waved her off.

She bowed and moved down the stairs, Ramonne's eyes on her full derrière the entire length of her descent. Slowly he turned back to Martin, running a hand through his thick mane. "Now you may speak, if you choose to."

Martin fumbled for the words. He was terrified, yet fascinated. This "creature" as the man referred to himself, obviously possessed hypnotic powers, and was, by his own witness, a cold-blooded murderer. Every instinct told Martin to flee, bolt from the table and run down the stairs.

But he sat transfixed by the man with the piercing eyes.

He composed himself. "What do you want from me?"

"*Au contraire*. It is you who have summoned me." Ramonne

savored the velvety claret, swirling it in the glass and watching it trail syrup-like down the sides.

"How so?" Martin was perplexed.

"Well, let's see if I can quote verbatim." Ramonne looked up whimsically at the ceiling. "'The Bangrak serial killer chooses his victims carefully, preying on the unfortunate have-nots, lost souls…women of the street or with a certain penchant for the loneliness of the wee hours.'" Ramonne leaned in close to Martin. "How did I do?" He sniffed again, and Martin recoiled.

Jesus. It's him!

"My God, man. You're insane."

"There you go again. I don't take particular offense, but *He* might, so I think I'd cool it on the name in vain thing. As for being *insane*, now that I do take umbrage to, sir." Ramonne sipped, his complete attention now devoted to the wine. "Beautiful, is it not?"

"Again, what do you want from me?" Martin didn't know what else to say. He was trapped in a booth on the second floor of a trendy nightspot with a serial killer who was savoring a 100-dollar bottle of Bordeaux. His world had collapsed.

Ramonne put down the glass and looked into Martin's eyes. Martin again felt the hypnosis, and tried to turn away. He couldn't.

"What do *I want*?" Ramonne hissed. "You insignificant worm. You 'expose' me after 150 years of anonymity, and you have the gall to ask *what I want*…?" The words were like steam from a kettle. "I truly don't want anything from you, Martin. Nothing, that is, but your mortal life."

Oh Jesus. Oh God. Help me.

"I warned you about using His name in vain, Martin. Believe me, neither He nor His Son can help you now." Ramonne leaned back in his seat and finished his glass.

He can read my thoughts.

"Yes. I can."

Oh fuck. What do I do?

"Listen to me. I will make it painless. Don't be afraid."

"Y-Y-Yes… Please don't hurt me."

"Martin, I said 'painless.' I still intend to kill you. Let's get that clear. But you know what…" He looked around, and, spotting the waitress, he motioned to her. "Let's make this fun. I know you fancy her."

When she arrived, Martin wanted to warn her, send her for the police; hell, send her for a pizza—just get her the fuck out of here. But again he couldn't say anything. He sat mute, like some poor fool, and watched Ramonne work his obscene magic.

The next minute, the next hour, the next four hours, the entire evening went by in a blur. Martin found himself a voyeur, a wallflower, as Ramonne seduced the girl, who promptly left her station, gathered her frock, and accompanied them out into the night. A taxi was procured, an anonymous hotel selected, and they walked unseen by the front desk and rode the elevator to the top floor. Ramonne prowled the hall until he detected an empty suite.

The penthouse had a balcony that overlooked Sukhumvit Road. Ramonne gently laid the girl on the massive bed and had what one would call 'missionary' sex with her. Martin watched, detached, almost somnambulant.

Ramonne then presented the girl to Martin, releasing him from his slumber.

Martin took the girl. He took her as though he had never had a woman before, and *fucked* her. The English language has a lot of words to describe this particular act of passion, but he *fucked* her…that described it best. When he was finished, he lay back and looked at her.

God, she's beautiful.

"Yes she is." Ramonne echoed his thoughts. "Now let me show you a woman's real essence… Excuse me." He moved Martin away, and he gently spread the young girl's silken thighs. Before Martin could protest, Ramonne bit down hard on her labia. He drew her lifeblood from her while she twisted and moaned in ecstasy. To Martin's astonishment, Ramonne levitated from the bed, lifting the girl with him. Her face contorted in an expression of complete rapture.

In minutes she was dead.

Martin shrank back, nauseous.

Ramonne straightened and wiped his lips. "Delicious, yes?" He set the lifeless form on the couch.

"You're a beast." Once again, Martin really didn't know what to say.

"Oh sure, *I'm* a beast. But I didn't see any hesitation on your part when it came to fucking her."

Intoxication. Martin felt it again. He knew he was once more under some sort of spell.

"This is your bonus, Martin. I'm granting you this little glimpse into my world so you can see what it's like to be me." He picked the girl up and onto his shoulder. "An existence that *you* would put an end to." He hoisted the girl onto the railing.

"*C'est la vie.*" He let the girl fall twenty stories into the traffic below.

———————

They walked through the crowds on Sukhumvit without attracting attention. Martin saw all the normal things—people, *tuk-tuks*, taxis, cars—passing by in a haze. His vision was blurred, unless he chose to clear it. Then, he found, he could focus on one face in the crowd, and it would become crystal clear. As the figures passed, Martin swore he could read their thoughts:

'Asshole, out of my way.'

'I really need a drink.'

'How much further?'

Soon they were on Soi 16. Ramonne led them down a side *soi* and to the deserted marsh surrounding Raja Lake. The city skyline towered in juxtaposition to the peaceful pond.

Martin focused on the water and found a school of catfish. They were far under the murky water, and yet to Martin they were as clear as they would be if the water was made of glass. He marveled at their sinewy movements.

"Time to die, my friend."

Martin found himself unable to offer any resistance.

"I think you'll drown. How does that suit you?" Ramonne tossed pebbles into the pond.

"It doesn't suit me at all," Martin managed.

Each time one of the pebbles broke the water's surface, the attending ripples seemed to spread across the lake in a rainbow of color.

Stall for time. Martin shook his head and tried to concentrate. "How old are you?"

"Well, let's see. I was born in 1825. That would make me 177 years young, as they always say. I look well, don't I?" He preened and posed.

"When did you become a…"

"A vampire…? Yes, that *is* the proper word for it." He smiled and reflected. "In 1860. June 17th to be precise."

"How?"

"I was bitten, of course." Ramonne smirked. "By another vampire, Martin."

"Where?"

"Where…? Geographically or physically?" He laughed.

"Where did it happen?" Keep stalling. Think of something.

"Angkor. In the Temple of Bayon. I was with the zoological expedition led by Henri Mouhot. We were exploring the tributaries of the Mekong River, and discovered the temples by accident in the Cambodian jungle. I was so excited by our 'discovery' that I couldn't wait for daybreak, and foolishly went at night to see the wondrous carvings by torchlight. I soon found the real reason why the Khmers had abandoned Angkor four centuries before. A very old Chinese vampire had decimated them. The subsequent landlords, Theravada Buddhists, secured an 'arrangement' with him, providing him with live-stock." Ramonne spat in disgust at the thought. "The monks and the vampire lived in relatively peaceful co-existence. But years of animal blood had made him weak, and when I stumbled upon him, he was a veritable shell of a beast. In his feeble state, he was unable to kill me, and left me to die a slow and agonizing death. My cries awakened something in him, and he granted to me the *gift*. Eternity. The endless life of the nocturnal hunter." He paused as the images of his memory flooded over him.

To Martin's absolute astonishment, he found that he too could *see* glimpses of the tale as Ramonne told it. The temple with its multitude of carved faces and intricate bas-reliefs, basking in the torchlight. The lagoon surrounding the temple shimmering in the moonlight...

"Monsieur Mouhot left me in charge of the exploration while he ventured further. Together, the old vampire and I destroyed my former colleagues. Oh, how we fed... For me those first meals were always the best. I was about to begin on the monks when he forbade me to feed on them; banished me to the jungle. I survived on snakes and rats, eventually reaching Siam and the city of Krung Thep where we now stand... But enough about me, let's get on with your demise, shall we?"

The wondrous images of ancient times vanished in a puff, and Martin found himself back in the present. 'In the moment,' as they say. His vision was restored to its former banal level. He no longer heard or saw Ramonne's thoughts. Ramonne had released his hold on him.

But as soon as the vampire had loosened his sensory grip, he grabbed Martin physically. He moved him to the water's edge and plunged Martin's head beneath the murky water.

Dear God. Don't let it end like this.

'Do you think God cares, Martin?'

The voice in his head was as clear as if it had been whispered directly to his ear.

'I'm rich. You can have it all.'

'I take what I need, Martin. I've no need for your pitiful wealth.'

'Twenty million dollars is hardly pitiful.'

Martin could hold his breath no longer. The foul water began to fill his lungs when he was suddenly lifted free into the blessed life-giving air.

"Twenty million *US?*" Ramonne asked, as Martin choked and gasped.

"Yes... Of course... US dollars. In a trust fund." Martin vomited...

But he was quickly plunged back into the water.

'A trust fund? Of what use is a trust fund to me?' Ramonne's voice echoed in his head.

'I control it. It's just set up that way to avoid taxation. It can be parceled out any way I see fit. Martin began to lose consciousness. Fuck. What a shitty way to die.'

And then he was back on dry land, Ramonne's hand on his chest, pumping him, forcing the fetid water out.

The vampire pinched Martin's nostrils and blew into his mouth. With the air came a scent of human waste and blood that instantly caused Martin to sit up and gag. Once again he vomited. He took quick, short breaths while his heart raced to the point of bursting.

"Aacchh!" Ramonne spat and wiped his mouth with a hand-kerchief that matched his shirt. "Now *that's* something I've never done before. *Disgusting.*" He spat again, while Martin slowly regained his life.

"Now tell me about this money and how it will become mine."

Martin explained, to Ramonne the vampire, that he was the only son of a very wealthy American. As a patent attorney, his father had been instrumental in protecting Bill Gates' propri-etorship of Microsoft, and had brokered a commission that appeared miniscule on paper, but when applied to the world-altering empire that Gates subsequently built up, proved to be a cash cow of such immense proportion that the only real problem facing Jonathan Larue and his heirs was how to spend it.

His father became a philanthropist of world stature, bequeathing stellar amounts of funding to museums and libraries and galleries in exchange for his name on a few bronze plates.

Martin had established various charities as a way of easing the guilt that came with his stress-free existence. This permitted his travels to sometimes have a greater purpose, but mainly he roamed the globe out of curiosity, and chose Bangkok as his base for its relatively easy access to Hong Kong and his bank account.

The ex-colony was a place he found less stimulating than the City of Angels, otherwise his *pied-à-terre* would probably be on Victoria Peak rather than Soi Lang Suan.

The sky was starting to turn blue around the edges when Martin finished his tale.

"Fascinating." Ramonne looked at the sky. "If I didn't possess eternal youth, I'd say I was jealous of you."

"*Touché.*"

'*I'm alive and I'm trading quips with a sarcastic vampire.*'

"All right, you can live… At least until I get your money." Ramonne started to walk.

"Hey, that sucks. Pardon the expression." Martin hurried to catch up with him. The vampire's stride was incredible, and he had to run to match it.

Suddenly, Ramonne stopped and turned on Martin. "So you'd prefer to die *now*?"

"Well no, of course not. I prefer not to die at all, if possible."

"That too, can be arranged." Ramonne walked on.

"That's *not* what I meant. Please, stop walking and talk to me."

Ramonne stopped and looked up. The sky was no longer black. "I have but a few minutes, *boy*." He sneered.

"What should I do?"

"Go home. Go to bed. Forget about this night. Especially forget about me. Speak to no one. Tonight we shall make further arrangements."

"Where?"

"At the Oriental Hotel. The Authors' Wing. Midnight." And then he was gone.

Martin's legs collapsed beneath him and he sank to his knees. And prayed.

8

That night, Martin awoke in a cold sweat. The sheets were soaked and lay crumpled in a ball at the bottom of the bed. He looked at the Sony Dream Machine: 8:00 p.m. He got out of bed and took a long shower, combed his hair and dressed.

When he got downstairs, Daeng had a pot of tea ready for him. She shook a packet of Equal into his cup and handed it to him. He immediately recognized the frown of disapproval. He chose the silent approach, and quietly sipped his tea.

After five minutes, Daeng couldn't hold back any longer. *"Pai nai maa. Meua keuan yuu tii nai?"* she snapped.

"I was out with an old friend." Martin replied.

"Old friend, ha! I parked the car and you never came upstairs for the next eight hours? Where was your 'old friend,' huh? Hiding in the bushes…? And where's the big German?"

"I ran into him in front of the building. We went for a drink. Hans went home."

"All night…? Some old friend. Tell me, your old friend got big tits?"

And with that she slammed the kitchen door and left him to drink his tea in silence.

———

Martin arrived at the Oriental by ten o'clock. Time enough to enjoy the delicious barbecue by the riverside and have a drink in the Bamboo Bar. The soft lights and cool jazz helped as he tried to make some kind of sense out of the previous night. But try as he might, there was no logic to any of it.

Face it. You spent the night with a vampire. A real, live, blood-sucking, 200-year-old monster. Well, not quite 200, but close enough. And why? Because you exposed him in an article you just had to write. He came to kill you. Together you lured a barmaid into a hotel and had sex with her, and then watched as he killed her. Oh, and what about that little incident with Hans? Can't forget old Headless Hans now, can we?

He decided that something a little stronger than club soda was in order, and caught the attention of the elegantly clad waitress. Only after she had delivered his drink did the irony of his ordering a Bloody Mary strike him, and he caused an American couple to turn his way when he laughed out loud.

And now what? I'm keeping an appointment with this monster, rather than getting on a plane. A plane to anywhere. Anywhere that doesn't have a blood-sucking ghoul who wants my considerable fortune and then to drown me in a putrid swamp.

Sweet Jesus, what's wrong with me?

He could hear Ramonne mocking him for his pious incantation.

Yet, that was the thing. He couldn't run away. In fact, he was actually excited about tonight. Except for the bloodletting of Hans and the girl, and the near-death experience of his own, last night had been…well…a *rush*. A kick.

He remembered the pungent aromas in the café, the scenes of ancient splendor that were conjured up when Ramonne spoke of the past. And *levitation*! My God, Ramonne had actually levitated when he sucked the life from the poor girl.

Yes. It was true. He *did* look forward to their encounter

tonight. Martin would be the first to admit that his fabulous wealth had made him jaded. He'd enjoyed more than his fair share of sexual adventures, his choice of Bangkok as his residence being testament enough to that. He'd tried opium dens and taken the Concorde to Paris for lunch. He'd lost an average man's annual salary on a turn of the wheel at Monte Carlo. And he was *fucking bored*!

Now, Ramonne…*he* was different. His was an existence full of wonderment. Martin was an old member of the Siam Society, and had attended numerous lectures on the history of Siam and the surrounding region. He'd been to Angkor many times, fascinated as he was with history and ancient cultures. But last night…*my God, I was there*…with Henri Mouhot and the discovery of the fabled temples.

Martin had received a taste of what the vampire could offer, and he wanted more.

————

The man stood with his hands on his hips, his noble face looking straight ahead, unafraid of the camera, while the young boy at his side had a cautious air about him. Both were dressed splendidly in pantaloons, silken blouse, with a tight gold vest. Their feet were fitted with elaborate sandals, and they were festooned with gold necklaces and rings. The man's hair was slicked back, and the boy's twisted into a topknot.

"Mongkut. Now *he* was a king!" Ramonne studied the sepia image closely, standing within inches of the glass.

Martin read the inscription on the brass plate below: RAMA IV, R. *1851-68*.

"But that Leonowens bitch ruined his great legacy with her fabrications and lies. *Anna and the King*, indeed."

The sitting room of the Authors' Wing was adorned with photos and drawings depicting Siam's recent history. Ramonne wandered the little gallery, his hands clasped behind his back and a smile on his face. Remembering.

The successive kings and their wives, consorts, sons, daughters, servants et al., were seen traveling abroad, arriving by steamer in Southampton, disembarking the liner in a circus-like procession complete with carriages both horse-drawn and horseless, and royal elephants—gifts from the monarch to his hosts.

Krung Thep was, at that time, a marvelous city of wide, tree-shaded avenues, criss-crossed by *klongs* or canals. Graceful barges plied their trade on the river. Everywhere were seen the smiles that the country is rightly noted for. A few pictures illustrated somber times during World War II and the Japanese occupation.

In 1950, a handsome, bespectacled young man was shown at his coronation, and the next fifty years of photos showed the nation coming of age under the guidance of its beloved king, Bhumibol.

Ramonne paused at a photograph, taken in Hollywood, of King Bhumibol visiting a soundstage with Elvis Presley. "Two kings," he mused…

Tonight the vampire wore another loose-fitting suit of light silk, and a collarless shirt with double rows of pearl buttons down the front. His shoes were soft, Italian leather, and he glided across the marble floor without a sound. He led Martin out past the pool to a table on the terrace overlooking the river.

A candle flame at their table danced in the light breeze, and almost as soon as they were seated, a waitress sank to her knees and took Ramonne's aperitif order: a '78 Lafite Rothschild. As she rose, bowed, and backed away, Martin realized that he hadn't seen Ramonne pay the bill last night.

"Do you have money?" Martin asked.

"Of course," Ramonne scoffed. "But perhaps not enough."

"Can you elaborate?"

"In my mortal state, I was from a titled family with property holdings in Provence. You are French, are you not?"

"My grandfather, yes," Martin replied. "I've been to Provence. It's beautiful."

"It *was*. Today…" Ramonne shrugged. "I wouldn't know. Anyway, I was presumed to have perished at Angkor along with the others—victims, the monks claimed, of a mysterious plague— though there was a problem when my corpse was not recovered. An insipid sibling was eventually able to lay deed to all my titles. However, before I left Angkor, I had the foresight to insert a last will and testament—indisputably writ in my own hand—amongst my personal possessions that were returned to France. This will stated my desire to form a trust in my name that would benefit the monastery ensconced in Angkor. I wisely stipulated that the trust's management was to be out of a bank in Krung Thep. Discovery of this document led to an endowment that has continued to this day."

"How do you withdraw the funds?"

"I wrote one letter in 1860 appointing a convenient host, whose identity I was assuming, and posted it from Krung Thep. My family assumed it was my last dying wish, and that this unfortunate soul and I had actually met and formed a pact. We'd met all right—but he was no more as a result."

"And this fund continues?"

"To this very day. I've invented a succession of worthy local administrators, and no one has ever bothered to come here and challenge its validity. But it has withered to a pittance. You can't believe the inflation of 140 years. It's shocking. I barely make ends meet."

"What if I may ask, are your expenses?"

The waitress arrived with the Lafite Rothschild. Martin knew the menu at the Oriental. It was a 200-dollar bottle. Ramonne swirled the rich vintage while the girl waited for his reaction. He pointed to the glass. "*This* is one of my expenses." He sipped and smiled at the waitress. "Superb."

She finished pouring and retreated to her station.

"Okay. Expensive wines. I understand that. But surely you must make up for that in the..." He searched for a delicate way to put it... "I mean you don't really *eat*, do you?"

Ramonne leaned forward. "No. I feed. My meals are free, in a manner of speaking."

"And, if I might ask, your lodgings?"

"My lodgings...? I sleep in a coffin. Not that it's any of your business." Ramonne scowled. "Your point being *what* exactly?"

"My point being that for most people, their major expenses are for food and lodging...two details you seem to have covered."

"What I do with my money is my own fucking business. You sound like my accountant." The vampire took a long drink of wine.

"I'm trying to get a picture of your situation, so I can help."

Martin knew that he was walking on eggs, but he'd thought this

through and was determined to go ahead with his plan. It was the only way he thought that he could save his own life.

Ramonne hissed. "You'll help when you give me your twenty million dollars."

"I'm afraid I can't do that." Martin swallowed as he said it.

"*Eh?*" In a flash the vampire was an inch from Martin's face. Martin hadn't seen him move.

"So you *do* want to die, then?"

"No. Of course not. It's just that...like you pointed out, a trust fund is complicated, and I can't just turn it all over—"

Martin suddenly *saw* his own death. Ramonne was once again plunging him into the swamp, and he was gasping for air. He tried desperately to wipe the image from his mind, but the vampire was feeding it to him, forcing it upon him.

"Not...not all at once, anyway."

The death scene disappeared.

"Not all at once?" Ramonne was puzzled. "Well, yes…I do suppose that would be difficult."

"Exactly. It would cause too many questions. Etceteras."

"Etceteras, etceteras." Ramonne was amused at the word. "Now. What are your other expenses—other than expensive red wines?"

"The police." He scowled. "If you must know, *that* is where most of my money goes."

"Bribes?"

"Of course, boy. Bribes. Baksheesh. Tea money. It's the grease that keeps the wheel turning. In my case, a large monthly stipend allows me to deposit as many bloodless corpses throughout this hell-hole as I have an appetite for."

Martin hated a man who appeared at least five years his junior calling him 'boy.'

Ramonne poured another glass.

"And they cover your tracks?"

"Like a vacuum cleaner. Regular bunch of Hoovers, those boys."

"How long has this been going on?"

"A *long* time. I'm greasing at least the third-generation of cop palms by now."

"Do they know you?"

"Only Boonsong knows me."

"Do you hunt only in Bangrak?"

"*Ha*! Do you think I exist on Bangrak alone? Do you know how often I feed, boy?" Ramonne scoffed as he finished the wine. "If I were to hunt in Bangrak alone, the streets there would look like medieval Europe…the black plague, bodies piled on every corner. No, I hunt all over. I spread my services throughout the kingdom."

Good Lord, I've dug up only the lid of the coffin.

"That's true," Ramonne said, reading Martin's fear. He signaled the girl over. "By the way, you're buying."

Martin smiled at the girl. "May I see the wine list please?"

Ramonne scowled and stopped her. He handed her the empty bottle. "Never mind that. We'll have another one of these."

"Of course."

When she left, Martin leaned toward Ramonne. "There *are* other acceptable wines…that are *much* more reasonable. Would you like me to show you."

"*You*? Teach me about wine? *Ha!* Boy, I've got wines that were brought into this harbor from France at the turn of the century— and I'm talking 1900, not the *new fucking millennium.*"

"Where do you keep those? Surely not in your coffin?"

"Don't mock me, boy. Of course not. I have a place. A *private* place. It holds my…my memories."

"So you do have assets?" Martin asked.

"Of course. I'm hardly a pauper."

"Have you ever thought of selling off these assets? The wine alone must be worth a for—"

"We are not here to talk about selling *off* my assets. Your impudence astonishes me. We're here to figure how you're going to give me *your* money."

"Of course. I'm merely trying—"

"Cut the bullshit. Where's your money?"

Martin tried *not to think* of the answer, but of course, he couldn't help himself.

"Hong Kong." Ramonne answered his own question. "I assume you draw it locally when you need it?"

"Yes. Hong Kong Bank, Sathorn Road branch."

"Well, I suggest tomorrow, you make a sizeable withdrawal —cash, of course—as a sign of good faith."

Good faith with a vampire? Martin found the thought amusing.

"Don't mock me, boy." Ramonne sneered.

"Would you please stop doing that?"

"What?"

"Reading my thoughts. It's very annoying."

"I can choose not to, if it pleases me."

"Well, please stop. It's very rude. And if we're going to be friends—"

"*Friends*? Who said anything about being friends?"

"I just thought…" *Treading on eggs.* "I just thought that if I give you my money, you should at least be—"

"I give you your life. Isn't that enough?"

"Well, no…actually, it's not." *Oh man, take it easy here.*

"*Really*? Martin, you do amaze me. What, pray tell, is it you want?"

Martin watched the girl uncork the fresh bottle, and he waited until she left before answering: "I want *more*. Last night you gave me a taste. I want more."

Ramonne slid Martin's glass to him. "Taste this."

Martin drank for the first time that evening, indelicately taking a long pull.

My God! I've never tasted anything so wonderful in my life.

At that instant, all the candles on every table came to life. Then thousands of tiny white lights appeared in all the trees, magically transforming the terrace with fairy-tale luminescence.

A gentle breeze blew the trees, and a heady aroma of jasmine and lilac wafted through the air and enveloped Martin. He breathed in deeply and let out a long, contented sigh. As if on cue, a flock of white doves crossed the moonlit sky.

Ramonne leaned back and smiled.

9

———————

Thus it was that an understanding was born between Martin and the vampire. Martin would give him money, and in exchange Ramonne would *show* Martin things. Wondrous things, magical things, and of course, *scary* things.

The next day, Martin went to his bank and withdrew 50,000 dollars. That night he met Ramonne at midnight, again, and handed him the cash. And then Ramonne spirited Martin to the grounds of Sanam Luang, and there outside the walls of the Grand Palace, described in vivid detail the coronation in 1868 of Chulalongkorn, the great king Rama V. Ramonne's descriptions came to life as, once again, he allowed Martin to *share* his memories.

Martin was left breathless, overwhelmed, and exhausted by the vampire's narrative skills, and was only brought out of his stupor by the callous way in which Ramonne took one of the many street prostitutes who plied their trade in the shadows of the royal park, devouring her on the spot, throwing her carcass into the bushes. Ramonne looked around for Martin. But Martin had fled the scene.

When Martin arrived at his apartment, Ramonne was

waiting outside. He stepped from the bushes, his yellow eyes glowing in the dim light.

"Martin."

Martin tried to ignore him. Tried to open the door to the lobby. But the vampire would not be ignored. He glided up the steps to where Martin stood.

"I won't hurt you, Martin."

"But the bloodletting... I can't take it."

"I know. You're human. Of course it repulses you." Ramonne touched Martin's hair, and Martin closed his eyes. "From now on, I will feed before we meet."

Martin opened his eyes. The vampire was gone.

———

In the coming weeks, Martin took to sleeping during the days and rising after dark. He awoke eager for his nocturnal forays. He continued his social calendar—he was usually ravenous at dinner, as it was now his only meal—but he always parted company with his friends by midnight. This was often awkward, for in Bangkok this was precisely the hour when many social events began. The carousing of the bars that most of his male friends considered a nightcap to a hearty meal, rarely took place before the witching hour. However, Martin would beg off with protests of a headache or an early morning, and then scurry away, his heart racing in anticipation of another night in the company of his nocturnal *friend.*

The vampire was a tireless and captivating narrator; Martin his enraptured audience. Soon they ventured into the sensual pleasures that were hinted at on their first night together. Ramonne took Martin to bordellos where, under the vampire's intoxicating spell, he experienced new levels of joy. They attended black-tie affairs of state, the vampire and his charge never once being questioned or denied admission. A single glance into Ramonne's eyes, and the doors were opened wide.

The vampire allowed Martin to share his seductive powers, taking women randomly and callously, sometimes two or three a night. Ramonne kept his desire for bloodletting in check, though it was evident to Martin that this was an almost impossible task.

They traveled the waterways of Ayutthaya, the former capital. To Martin's wide-eyed amazement, stone ruins were restored to their former splendor. Torchlight illuminated golden temples during the *Loy Kratong* festival, where beautiful women and young children marched in procession to the waterfront and launched hundreds of banana-leaf rafts with candles onto the tranquil water.

In Bangkok they hung from ledges atop skyscrapers, and spied on their residents. They hid in the shadows of the city's many bridges, read the minds of passers-by, and laughed at the absurdity of human life.

"You hear that?" Ramonne queried on one occasion as they sat under the Rama IX Bridge. He passed a bottle of Bordeaux to Martin.

Martin listened. With the vampire's ears as his guide, he *heard* the sound of rap music. A young man with headphones on, was crossing the bridge.

"Sometimes I'll choose a victim just because of *that*."

"Because of what?"

"What they listen to. You mortals are given a fleeting moment, a speck of time. How dare you waste it listening to that?"

"You're the judge?" Martin passed the bottle back.

"Judge and jury." Ramonne stood. "Music is part of life's essence. Like water to you, blood to me. Without it you wither and die."

"What else?"

"What *else*?" Ramonne drained the bottle and tossed it.

"Life's essence. You said music was a part of it. What else is essential?"

"Well, as you and I both know, sex is essential. It sustains the soul."

"'The soul?' You talk of soul?"

"Of course. Do you think I'm soulless? I attained eternal life. I didn't relinquish my soul."

"But I thought—"

"'Damnation?' Hell? Brimstone? Do I look like I'm damned? Boy, I only started to live when that wretched old beast attacked me. I relish the time I've gained. I cherish the night and the gifts it brings me."

"Okay. Sex and music. What else?"

"Don't be flippant. Like music, sex has many forms. There's opera. There's jazz. There's pure unbridled lust. There's straight fornication. And then...then there's love."

"You constantly amaze me."

"It's been a long time, Martin. But once, I knew true love. That has been the greatest sacrifice...I gained eternal life, but I lost true love."

"So, you have regrets."

"A life without regrets is a life not lived. If I have one regret, I have a thousand blessings. I'm immortal, Martin. You and this claptrap generation of eager beavers will pass in the blink of an eye. But I...I will remain."

For a moment Ramonne seemed to lose his arrogance. He stared off and didn't speak.

"I will remain, always."

"You'll see us to our graves."

Ramonne smiled. "Many I will *put* in their graves."

"And then the next generation."

"And the next. Ad infinitum... Forever." He sighed. "Come on, boy. Before the sun rises."

———

Daeng was beside herself at Martin's new habits. She would try to rouse him from his heavy slumber, to no avail. When he did rise, he had little time for her. Whatever romance had been in their life was a thing of the past.

Martin treated her coldly, but still asked her to run errands, one of which included a trip to an immigration attorney with his passport and a sum of cash. To her surprise, Martin received the first non-tourist visa she'd ever known him to possess. He was now permitted to reside in the kingdom, undisturbed, for ninety days. This was followed soon after by his instructions to cancel his myriad travel plans. He had her make cash withdrawals from his account, while he slumbered the days away. Her questions were met with vague replies.

Daeng knew Martin was in trouble; she just didn't know what to do about it.

And then Martin got the second response to his article.

10

Daeng returned home one afternoon from a 'bank run,' as Martin had now taken to calling his repeated plundering of his own resources. She had 30,000 dollars in 1,000-baht notes in her purse, and she was understandably nervous. She practically jumped out of her skin when she exited the private elevator that brought her directly from the car park to their apartment, and was confronted by a young, foreign stranger outside her very door.

"How did you get in here?" she demanded, clutching her bag.

"Easy. Simmer down," the young man replied. "The door was open downstairs."

"Impossible. There's a guard." Daeng fumbled for her key.

"Must be on a break." He shrugged. "Anyway, I'm looking for Martin Larue."

Instinctively, she lied: "Never heard of him. This my place." She stuck the key in the lock.

"Funny. His name's on the registry downstairs. This *is* 7A?"

She had the door open and quickly darted inside. "Go away!"

She slammed it shut. Slammed it on his big American foot.

He let out a howl of pain, and Daeng reflexively opened the door. In a moment he was in.

Now she really was scared. "Martin! *Martiiiiinnnn!*"

Her cries cut through Martin's slumber. He flung off the sheet and stumbled naked into the hall. "Daeng? *What's wrong?*"

"Martin Larue?" the stranger calmly inquired.

"Yes?" Martin tried to cover himself.

"Jonathan Peyton. We need to talk…"

———

Martin dressed while Daeng served Jonathan a Singha beer on the screened-in terrace. Seven floors allowed a clear view of the sun descending over Lumpini Park.

Martin emerged from the bedroom and stood in the arched entry and studied Jonathan Peyton…

California.

He wore baggy khaki pants with a multitude of pockets, and white leather walking shoes…

Probably LA.

His Hawaiian shirt was a vintage pattern generated by a store in Honolulu that Martin knew well. His blond hair was at an inbetween-stage, not long ago cropped fashionably short, but now growing out. He had a slight tan, and even though he was indoors, he wore sunglasses…

Definitely Los Angeles.

"How do you like Bangkok?" Martin asked as he stepped into the room.

"Fascinating city," Jonathan remarked.

Martin sat down. "First visit?"

"No. Second."

"What brings you here?"

"You."

Martin squinted as Jonathan unfolded a three-page document that revealed itself as an Internet print-out of the *Bangkok*

Times article. It was well worn from handling, and was about to rip.

"Really? I had no idea that we reached such a wide audience." Martin tried to view the document with detachment. "Daeng, would you run down to the corner for some more beer. I could use one myself."

She looked at him with suspicion. "We have plenty."

"I prefer Heineken. Maybe Mr. Peyton does, too."

Daeng scowled and left the room.

"Where are you from, Mr. Peyton?"

"Chicago. And call me Jonathan, please... I subscribe to a service that scans the press in Southeast Asia for articles that match the parameters I give them. Yours fit the profile."

"Really? What profile is that?" Martin tried to remain calm.

Jonathan took a sip from his Singha and set the bottle on the coaster. "Serial killings, for starters. Young female victims, perhaps. But most of all, macabre. Corpses drained of their blood." He leaned toward Martin and said in a hushed tone, "Vampires."

Martin tried to appear amused. "Vampires...?" He sniggered. "Oh, come now. What nonsense."

"Not nonsense, Mr. Larue. Not nonsense, I assure you." He withdrew an envelope from his hip pocket. Inside were a half dozen color snapshots. He handed them to Martin.

Oh, Christ. Not more.

They were pictures of corpses. A young woman. A young man. An old, bearded man. Their pallor was chalky white. The last two were of a beautiful woman. There were scratches on her throat and her side. In the final picture there were the now-familiar streaks of blood down her naked thighs.

"Look familiar?" Jonathan asked.

"They're grotesque... Horrible." Martin handed the photos back. "But what do they have to do with me?"

"The method of killing. These all took place within a two-week period. This last one…" He held up the beautiful naked woman. "That's my wife. We were married a week."

"My God. I'm sorry."

"The beast attacked us in our hotel, the Royal Cliff in Pattaya. We were on our honeymoon. We'd married in Hawaii, I had some business in Hong Kong, and Thailand seemed right in the middle. Jennifer was a great traveler. Anything different turned her on. We spent two nights in Bangkok and then went down to Pattaya. The hotel sits on a cliff, quite secluded. Do you know it?"

Martin nodded. He knew it well. It was the only place he could abide in Pattaya.

"We'd had a fabulous time. Boat rides, parasailing, jet skis, all the silly beach crap on a private island the hotel charters. Nights, we mostly spent around the hotel, you know."

Martin knew. He'd never been married—never saw the point really—but he could imagine what a honeymoon was like.

"We had a private villa with a pool. Very nice."

And expensive. Jonathan Peyton had some money.

"The bedroom was upstairs. We were getting ready for bed. The night was gorgeous. The moon was on the wane, but it was crystal clear. Suddenly, this man, this *beast* leaps through the bay window, shattering the glass. He goes straight to my wife, and without the slightest effort, throws her over his shoulder. I shout at him to stop, but he backhands me like he's a swatting a fly. I crashed into the bureau and was stunned. He leaped through the broken window to the ground, twenty feet below. I staggered to the opening and saw him sprint across the lawn, with Jennifer over his shoulder.

"I grabbed the phone and blurted out that my wife had been kidnapped. Thank God the girl understood me and phoned the police. I ran downstairs and across the garden. The monster was at the edge of the cliff. A chasm, over thirty feet wide, separated it from another spit of land. On the other side, it dropped straight to the sea. I yelled for Jennifer. The monster looked back at me. And then, with her still over his shoulder, he *leaped* across that canyon. Jesus! I could not fucking believe it."

Martin could. But he remained quiet.

"I raced back to the hotel. All hell was breaking loose, but not fast enough for me. I grabbed a security guard's pistol and knocked a startled bellboy off his motorbike and tore after him. I'd rented a bike earlier in the week and knew there was a road up to the other side of the canyon. I raced there as fast as I could, but got confused in the dark and it took me ten minutes to find the road.

"I went as far as I could with the bike, and then ran into the brush on foot. It took another ten minutes of stumbling through thick briars to find him. He had an altar, a huge slab of stone in a clearing, and he had Jennifer stretched out on it. She was naked and his head was between her thighs."

Jonathan turned to Martin, who was suddenly glad of the sunglasses. He didn't want to see Peyton's eyes.

"He was drinking her blood, Mr. Larue. This monster was drinking my wife's blood. I fired at him from no more than twenty feet. He spun around as the bullet hit him, and threw my wife aside like a rag doll. I fired again and again. I hit him, but it didn't stop him. He leaped on me and his teeth gashed my throat."

Jonathan pulled his collar open, and two marks were visible. "I fought with him. I emptied the gun point blank into his chest, but he was impossible to shake off and I was growing weaker.

"Just then, a police helicopter rose over the bluff, and a white-hot searchlight bathed us both in its glare. He released me and leaped off the cliff."

He closed his shirt collar. "We were on a point overlooking the sea. It was a 200-foot drop, straight down to the waves crashing on the rocks below. They never saw him again. No body was ever found."

He picked up his beer. "I was air-lifted to Bangkok. I was in intensive care for five days, and had four transfusions. I nearly died. My wife…" He looked away. "She was dead."

"Again. I'm so sorry." Martin didn't know what else to say.

"The police admitted to me that this had been the work of a serial killer. They told me of the other deaths I showed you. But they were convinced that he had fallen to his death and been swept out to sea. No one, they assured me, could survive a fall like that, let alone the amount of gunshots I described. That was it. Their case was closed."

"I'm so sorry."

"He *leaped* off that cliff. He didn't fall… I stayed in Thailand for two more months. I waited for the beast to strike again. But he never did. Finally I went home. That was over a year ago. I've been searching for him, but he hasn't surfaced…until now." He turned away from Martin and watched the lights of the city begin to twinkle against the purple sky.

Martin wondered. "You called him a vampire. What was the police's reaction to that?"

"What do you think…? But tell me, what else could it be?"

Daeng returned with the beer and poured one for Martin. "Here's your *Heineken…honey*." She went back to the kitchen.

Martin left the glass where it was.

———

That night, Martin made his usual rendezvous with Ramonne. They met at Wat Arun, the Temple of Dawn on the banks of the Chao Phraya opposite the Grand Palace. The 200-foot-tall *prang* was embedded with ceramics and porcelain from Chinese merchant vessels. At night it was lit from below, and Martin spotted Ramonne seated halfway up the tower. He begrudgingly made the climb and sat next to the vampire.

"See it, Martin. This is the finest view of Krung Thep. In 1882, I followed the great photographer Baron Raimund von Stillfried to this very spot. His camera captured the panorama you see below. Of course, the waters were cleaner then, and the harbor was full of tall ships. Dozens, with their graceful masts. They lay at anchor, their every need catered to by a floating market of hundreds of sampans filled with fruits, vegetables, and supple young girls."

Ramonne regaled Martin with his tales, and Martin listened, but with a detached ear. He was distracted, and barely gave a thought to Ramonne's incantations, the result of which meant that he literally failed to *see* what he was saying. Finally, unable to contain himself any longer, he interrupted: "Have you ever been to Pattaya?"

Ramonne was still in the late nineteenth century, and had to transport himself into the present. "Pattaya...?" He narrowed his eyes, uncertain of his reply. "Why?"

"Just curious."

"Hmmmm." Ramonne studied Martin. They had reached an agreement, of sorts, about the thought-reading thing, and he had got out of the habit of tuning into Martin's gray matter all the time, but perhaps it was necessary to reconsider this, now that he had raised this accusation.

"Don't," Martin commanded.

"I beg your pardon?"

"Don't read my thoughts...please. Just answer the question."

"Well, don't we sound like a couple of old queens? Don't do this, don't do that."

"Would you just answer my question?"

"How much is it worth to ya?" Ramonne sneered.

"Oh, God. You've gotten a quarter million dollars from me in the past three weeks. Would you just answer my fucking question?"

Ramonne capitulated. "Okay. Yes. I've been to Pattaya. So what? Is that a crime?"

"*Everything* you do is a crime... Oh, God. It *was* you."

"What? What did I do?"

"What did you do? You went on a rampage that ended up with six people dead."

"Did not. I was merely a tourist. I rented a car."

"You drive?" Martin was surprised.

"Boy." He sneered. "You forget that I saw the fucking things invented. Of course I don't *drive*." He spat the word out in disgust. "I had a driver. Two, in fact. One to get me there and one to bring me home. They were both delicious as I recall."

Martin didn't laugh. "And?"

"I went out of town to get away from the cops. They said I was making Bangkok too hot. Ha! There's irony for you. So I went to the beach. While I was there, I had to feed, didn't I?"

"Yeah. You fed, all right. No cutting back 'cause you might arouse a few suspicions… ? Nothing like that ever entered that demented vampire brain of yours did it?"

"Martin. Cool it."

"I will not cool it. The husband of your last victim there was an American. He read my article. Now he thinks his wife's killer is in Bangkok."

Ramonne was furious. "Do you see? I told you your article would make trouble for me. Is making trouble for me. And Boonsong's bleeding me dry."

"Nice metaphor." Martin shook his head.

Ramonne calmed. "Thank you. It just came out that way… Ever since your fucking newspaper story, he's been demanding ten times the old pay-off. Or he'll expose me. I'm thinking of eating him. The little prick." He twisted his face into a rather hideous grimace.

"I'm sure you'll find a way to deal with Boonsong. But what about this self-appointed vampire hunter from Chicago?"

Ramonne closed his eyes. And he remembered… He was back on the bluff in Pattaya. Martin, unfortunately, was too.

"Stop!" Martin shouted. "I don't want to know this."

But Ramonne didn't stop. The images flowed. The frightened, innocent girl, swept away. The impotent husband firing his puny weapon, its slugs only diversions as the vampire turned on him, having already ravaged the woman. And then the life-threatening brightness of the helicopter's searchlight as it rose over them.

"Enough!" Martin shouted again.

The images faded. Ramonne turned to Martin. "He wants to come here? To find me?"

"Yes."

"Encourage him. It's a job I need to finish."

Martin decided it was best not to tell Ramonne that Jonathan Peyton was already in Bangkok. "This is all so unbelievable."

"Get over it, boy. You've known me for what…three weeks? Do you think you understand me?" Ramonne scowled. "Look. Why do you think I let you live, you impudent little fuck? I relate to you. I want to roam the world at will. But I remain in Bangkok. It's home." Ramonne paced on the tier of the *chedi*. "Every once in a while I go a few hundred miles to take the heat off. It's good for me to disappear for a while."

"Where do you go?"

"All over the kingdom. Kanchanaburi, Chiang Mai. Wherever my fancy takes me. Just like you."

"You don't have to lug your coffin around with you?"

"Of course not. I prefer my coffin, mind you. Nothing like the sleep I get there. But it's certainly not a requirement." Ramonne sat down again. "I dream of night flights to Tokyo. You know, the red-eye? I'd sleep the day at the airport in one of the comfortable little capsule hotels—which are very much like coffins, as you know—then journey on at night to any of hundreds of ports. But I'm afraid. All it takes is one bomb scare some place, and I'm sitting on the runway for eight fucking hours and the sun's coming up. Travel these days is so risky." He yelled at a passing longtail boat, and it slowed and turned to the dock.

"You know something about me, Martin. But there is so

much more." He moved close. "And you'll never really know it all until you commit."

"Commit?" Martin was puzzled.

"Become a vampire, Martin. I know you want to. I will do it for you."

"What?"

"Do it, Martin. I offer you my gift."

The longtail skipper looped a rope over a piling and waited.

"Think of it, Martin. How else will you get to spend that obscene endowment of yours? You know what they say…'you can't take it with you.'"

Without another word, Ramonne leapt off the tower, landing like a cat from the 100-foot drop. Without speaking to the astonished boatman, he climbed in and they sped off into the night.

11

"Mr. Peyton…sorry, Jonathan. You mentioned you had business in Hong Kong. What do you do?"

Martin and Jonathan were seated on the patio of DeliFrance, at the entrance to the Central Towers office complex on Silom Road. The early evening crowd passing by consisted mainly of well-groomed young women in tight, short skirts, secretaries on their way home. Jonathan's hotel was around the corner, and the café was suggested by Martin as much for its convenience as its view.

"I'm a publicist. I handle the Chicago Philharmonic, among others. I have a small firm, just three employees, in an old art deco building on Michigan Avenue. It provides me with a good, reliable income. Unlike many businesses today, I'm not at the mercy of the economic climate. If you need a publicist now, you'll always need one. It virtually runs itself and gives me lots of freedom." He sipped his café au lait. "The *freedom* I need to pursue this monster."

Martin was hesitant to ask, but he did: "What's your plan?"

"I had hoped to meet with the Bangrak police, but they stonewalled me, vehemently denying any truth to your story."

Martin was hardly surprised.

"Look, you're my only real hope here. You know what I've said is true. The same beast that killed my wife is here…killing and feeding, indiscriminately for ten years or more."

A lot more.

"I really don't know what I can do. I just reported a story."

"Tell me how you put the story together. There are clues there, I assure you."

"I don't know what I can do."

"Please. I'm begging you."

Martin took a deep breath. Every fiber of his being resisted, but he felt compelled to tell at least part of his tale.

No vampire. No mention of Ramonne.

He started with Prakasan's summons to his office. In telling the tale, Martin was taken back to his time of innocence. Before meeting the vampire. Before being seduced by the vampire. Before… The rest was unthinkable.

And yet, since Ramonne's offer, Martin had been unable to sleep. Unable to eat. Unable to think of anything else. His analytical mind actually tried to weigh the pros and cons of it. *Pros and cons? We're talking eternal damnation.* One side spoke out. *We're talking eternal life! Not some pathetic seventy-year existence of pain, misery, and uncertainty, culminating in the graceless collapse of your feeble body. We're talking eternal youth!*

Martin had to remind himself that he wouldn't get any younger, but he would remain 41 forever—and that part of it was perfectly acceptable. What *wasn't* acceptable was the…*what did Ramonne call it…? The hunt?*

The taking of human life, coldly, mercilessly…*eternally!*

"The first girl…I saw her that night in Hernando Cemetery." Martin recalled his retching horror at seeing that first naked corpse in the mausoleum. He saw her upside-down eyes. Her contorted smile. The dried blood on her thighs. The beast that could do such a thing was beyond comprehension to him then. Yet, now…that beast was a part of his life. *That beast* is *my life now.*

"The girl appeared in the papers a week later. They said she'd drowned."

Jonathan watched, concerned, as Martin struggled. His mind flooded with images. The black and white photos of the victims atop the tomb. Ramonne taking the waitress on their first night together, his head between her legs, the two of them levitating off the bed. His face turning to Martin…his mouth smeared with blood…his yellow eyes burning. And then their nightly forays together…passion, wonder… Amazement.

Before him sat the end of that life. Jonathan Peyton was here in Bangkok on a mission to destroy a vampire. Not just any vampire.

My vampire!

Martin's head began to spin. He felt nauseous, though he hadn't eaten or drank anything. Maybe that was it…he hadn't eaten for three days. He clutched the table and pulled the starched white tablecloth to the floor with him as he collapsed in a shatter of glass and breaking plates.

Twenty-five stories above them, Ramonne stood watching, his hair blowing in the breeze. As Martin collapsed, he turned his back to him. He slowly crossed the tar-paper roof and descended to the car park.

12

Tubes. That's odd. I have tubes in my arms.

Martin came to in a thirteenth-floor suite of the very plush Bumrungrad Hospital. 'Suite' was the appropriate description, as the hospital was known worldwide for its five-star accommodations. Muted lighting, marble floors, teak shutters…all were standard throughout, giving the hospital the ambience of a first-class hotel.

"Martin? You awake?"

Daeng was seated next to the bed, and as Martin turned to her, she rose and brushed his matted hair off his forehead.

"What happened?" He found it difficult to speak.

"You collapsed. Dehydration, the doctor said. He also said you needed nourishment, but I told him you were like a bear—plenty of fat to live on."

Martin tried to smile. It hurt. His lips were parched and cracked. He reached for a glass of water. A needle in the back of his hand stopped him. It hurt, too.

Daeng held the glass of water for him, and put the flex-straw to his mouth.

She smiled at him. "Martin. What's going on?"

He turned away, wanting to cry. Yet he didn't know why.

He turned back. "Daeng, I…I can't answer that just yet. But I will." He looked at the concern, the fear in her sweet dark eyes, and wanted to cry again. "I promise you. But now I just want to sleep."

He closed his eyes and kept the tears to himself. The way his father had taught him.

———

It had been dark for two hours when Ramonne arrived at the hospital. He had no problem with visiting hours. Such restrictions did not apply to those who could cloud men's minds. He passed through the reception areas undetected, and entered Martin's room.

Immediately Martin felt his presence.

He sat up in the bed as Ramonne approached.

"Hospitals. Wonderful places. Full of blood, full of life…and death."

The vampire breathed in deep, and Martin *felt* it. Hundreds of stories swept past him in an instant; all the people that had occupied this room, *this bed*, washed over him… Births, deaths, loss, gain, the ever changing balance on the scales of life—it was all here.

He looked at Martin. A look, perhaps, of pity. "It saddens me to see you this way."

The tears were brimming, and this time Martin let them flow.

"I'm ready."

"So you are," Ramonne answered. "But not tonight. Not here."

Ramonne put his hands over Martin's bloodshot eyes and closed them. In the dark, Martin heard his soft, yet firm voice.

"Go home and wait."

"When?" Martin whispered.

Ramonne didn't look at Martin as he replied. He stared straight ahead. A steely coldness in his eyes.

"Soon, I promise you."

Martin wept like a child. Unashamed. Unabashed. Unrepentant.

13
___

The Democracy Monument extended its stylized hands into the night sky in a sacred *wai*. Traffic circled non-stop around the giant sculpture.

In its shadow, a police car was parked at the entrance to a small park. Sergeant Thamarat came through the gate. His driver flicked a cigarette and started the car. The sergeant paused before getting in. He turned to the shadows and spoke: "I'm just a messenger. But the message is clear… Do it."

Ramonne stayed back, fire in his eyes.

The police car pulled out into the traffic and sped away.

___

Another rooftop. Another city view.

The vampire—perched on a ledge—swigged from a bottle of wine. His eyes were cold…distant. The wine ran down the corners of his mouth, leaving red stains. He finished the bottle and then flung it into the night.

He wiped his mouth with the back of his hand and stood. Arching his head back he howled.

The sound of an animal in great pain.

Martin went home. And waited…for hour after monotonous, flatulent, repetitive hour.

He hid away in his room, watching TV. Movies only. The news, current affairs, had no meaning to him. He avoided all who called. Especially Jonathan.

Especially Jonathan.

And waited.

Finally it came. Not a fax. Not an e-mail. Not even a phone call. Daeng handed Martin the thick parchment envelope with the wax seal on the back. *M. Larue* was neatly lettered by hand on the front, in fine calligraphic style.

"Thanks." Martin was anxious to open it, but he wanted Daeng to leave.

"Old friend?" she asked pointedly.

"Yes," Martin replied.

"I'll leave you alone." And she did, slamming the door on her way out.

He used his father's Fuller Brushman letter opener to slit the seal. Inside the envelope was a matching parchment note that simply said:

Tonight. Midnight. Hernando.

It was signed with the initial "R."

Tonight. My God. Tonight. What do I do?

He quickly decided there was nothing to do. All of that would happen *after*.

He fumbled in his drawer for matches, and lit the corner of the note. He dropped it into a steel waste bin and did the same with the envelope. It burned with a blue flame.

"Tonight." He repeated it over and over.

14

When he arrived just before the allotted hour, the cemetery was closed, the gate locked. Just as he was thinking what kind of cruel prank this was, the rusty gate swung open of its own accord.

Jesus! Mental manipulation of solid, inert objects.

"No. That is not possible," Ramonne answered as he stepped into the lamplight touching the gate. "Come." He rested a hand on Martin's shoulder.

Instantly, Martin felt warm and comfortable. The graveyard was particularly pleasant, and he was delighted to be there. He followed his friend into the mausoleum.

Inside, the most beautiful girl he had ever seen lay naked atop the marble. Martin was instantly aroused. His whole being was a sexual organ, and he had to—*had to!*—have her.

"That's it, Martin. She's yours." Ramonne smiled as Martin shed his clothes and climbed atop the girl.

She swooned as Martin entered her. She was quite obviously *intoxicated.* She rose and fell with his passions. Martin shuddered as he released his seed deep within her.

"Fine," Ramonne commented as Martin lay motionless on

the girl, spent. She continued to move, slowly, rhythmically, to some other master.

Martin looked back at Ramonne, who produced the knife with the serrated edge that he had used on Hans.

"Here, Martin."

Martin removed himself and rolled off the girl. She continued to writhe, under a spell.

Ramonne handed him the knife. "Be strong, boy. Carve her. Cut the bitch."

Martin looked at the knife, then at the girl. He moved to her...And stopped.

Why? Why like this?

"Oh, come on, boy." Ramonne grabbed the knife and slashed the girl between the legs...

Once.

Twice.

He opened her so her blood flowed like water. But she continued to twist and moan in ecstasy

"Now drink, Martin." He hesitated and Ramonne pushed him into the girl. "Drink."

Martin fell to his knees.

Why? Why like this? This is not right. This is not—

"Silence," Ramonne commanded. "Do as I say."

Martin felt the blood seeping over him, staining him, as he knelt between her legs. He tried to rise, but Ramonne held him there.

Then a voice rang out. "Stop!"

Instantly, Ramonne's hand disappeared from Martin's neck. A light—horribly bright—blinded Martin as he turned to the source of the voice. He felt powerful hands pull him from the girl. At the same time as he felt the vampire's release, his senses returned to normal.

"Martin Larue, you are under arrest for murder."

Returned to *hell*.

Naked, blood-soaked, his hands cuffed behind his back, Martin stared up at the cold face of Lieutenant-Colonel Boonsong. He tried to speak, but a billy club whipped across the back of his skull.

15

This time, Martin awoke in a filthy cell, wrapped in a thin, worn blanket. His clothes, minus his belt and shoes, were piled in the corner. To his horror, he discovered he was covered in caked, dry blood. There was a pail of water and a bowl next to a hole in the ground that would be his toilet. He poured water over his aching head, feeling the egg-sized lump on the back. He scrubbed at the darkened blood, and it washed off him in pink rivulets. He dressed and sat in a corner.

Pedestrians passed the small slat of a window six feet over his head; so he was in a basement. And it was day, as a thin shaft of sunlight pierced the bars of his cage. His was one of a half dozen small cells that lined each side of a narrow corridor. He could make out other hapless souls in the shadows of their confines, and there was a low, steady murmur of voices. At the end of the corridor a guard dozed at a metal desk.

What the fuck happened to me? Martin tried not to succumb to the fear and panic that were rising inside his chest...

As the sun began to recede, by Martin's calculation probably ten hours from the time he'd woken, he received his first and only meal of the day. A man in tattered gray pajamas pushed a cart down the aisle, dolloping rice gruel into the bowls that each prisoner extended eagerly through the bars. Martin fished his bowl out of the water and held it out.

The food was disgusting but he ate it...

———

"Sign it." The taught-faced man in a rumpled suit pushed the three-page document to Martin.

Martin scanned the first few lines and pushed it back. "*Mai.* I read Thai and I won't sign that."

It was a full confession to not only the murder of the girl that he had been caught with, but also to the other slayings at the Hernando Cemetery. Listed as evidence was the bone-handled knife with Martin's fingerprints. Martin's semen was documented as evidence of the brutality of the crime. Now, he was not just a serial murderer, he was a serial murderer-rapist.

It was his third day in prison, and this was the first official he'd seen other than the guards that kept watch at the end of the corridor. He had been roused from his sleep and taken to a vault-like room with a metal table, an old fan, and an overhead lamp. A uniformed guard stood behind Martin, and smacked his head each time he pushed the paper back to the man in the suit.

"I'm an American citizen. I demand to see a representative from the US Embassy."

"Ha! You want one phone call, too? You're not in America now. You're in Thailand. Sign this and you can see whomever you like. Maybe George Bush. Ha." The man slid the paper across the table again.

Martin folded his arms. He would not sign.

He spent three more days in the relative solitude of his cell. His attempts to make friends with the other prisoners were met mostly with mute indifference. He was a *farang,* and as such not to be trusted. One wretched old man did tell him where he was. He wasn't in a prison as such, but in a holding cell beneath the Bangrak Police Station. He would be held until he went to trial. The old man had been there for two years.

In the wretched misery of an endless week locked in a cage, Martin tried to piece together the events that had brought him here, and what went so very wrong.

What went wrong? You wanted to become a vampire, you fucking idiot, that's what went wrong.

In some strange way, some bizarre twist of fate had saved him from himself. If one could look upon waking up in a squalid prison a blessing, Martin reasoned that he had received a sign. God had intervened with his blasphemous plan.

Martin wept in silence. And thanked God for rescuing him.

"You. Up!"

Martin got to his feet as the guard opened the door. The man gave him an obligatory shove, and Martin went down the corridor, past the vaulted inquisition room, and up the stairs to a room where the brightness nearly blinded him. After a week in the grim holding cell, the lime-green walls and white fluorescent light were jarring. He squinted as he adjusted to it.

"Down!" The guard pushed Martin onto a stool facing a chicken-wire fence.

It was Daeng.

"Martin! My God! What have they done to you?"

Martin opened his eyes and saw her through the mesh. "Daeng. Thank God." He put his fingers through the wire and touched hers. It was the first real human contact he'd had in a week.

He was overjoyed, even before he realized that Prakasan was seated next to Daeng.

"Khun Prakasan. Very good of you to come. How on earth did you find me?"

"Daeng called me. She thought I'd sent you on another 'stupid' story, as she put it… Martin, I'm so sorry."

Martin smiled weakly. "It's not your fault."

"I was immediately suspicious of Boonsong, but it took four days to even get an admission that he was holding you. It took two more days to get us in to see you."

"Does the embassy know?"

"They do now, yes. You should be able to see a representative shortly. But, Martin, they told me not to expect much from them. In a murder case, their hands are tied. They can only see that you are granted justice according to Thailand's laws…very different from your own."

Daeng shook her head at the mention of the word 'murder.' "Martin. How could you?"

"I didn't, Daeng. I was set up." He wasn't sure she believed him. He wasn't sure that she should. He'd been a bastard to her, and he wanted more than anything to tell her how sorry he was. But there would be time for that later. Hopefully.

"Khun Prakasan. Write this down."

Prakasan took a notebook and a pen from his pocket. Martin gave him a name and a phone number. "Call him. He'll know what to do."

"Time." The guard pulled Martin to his feet.

"Daeng. I'm sorry."

The guard opened the door to the stairwell and shoved Martin toward it. Before he could say any more, the man pushed him through and he stumbled down the stairs…

———

Within 48 hours, Martin walked out of Bangrak Police Station. As is often the case with a man of considerable means, Martin's money separated him from the wretched proletariat.

The name and number he had given Prakasan was that of a powerful French attorney who practiced and taught law in Thailand. He had written books on Thai law, in Thai, and was one of the very few *farangs* to have actually secured a deed in his own name to property in the kingdom. He had an estate on the island of Phuket in the south, and Martin had been his guest on numerous occasions. The attorney had demanded and got an immediate hearing on Martin *in absentia*, in which he successfully negotiated Martin's release on the forfeiture of a two-million-dollar bond. Money talked and Martin walked.

Daeng and Prakasan accompanied Martin and his lawyer out of the station. A driver held the door of the limo for them.

The lawyer's advice was straightforward: "Martin, I suggest you leave the country immediately, and never return."

It was standard practice in Thailand for anyone who posted a significant bail bond to flee the scene. To do otherwise would have been an aberration. Even Martin could imagine the headline in the *Bangkok Times*: MURDER SUSPECT DOESN'T SKIP BAIL.

"Of course, you'll forfeit the bond," the attorney said matter-of-factly as he handed Martin his passport. The court would keep the bond without having to go through the whole bother of a trial. Everyone would be happy.

"The money's not important." Martin sighed.

"It'll save your life," Prakasan urged.

Martin pressed a button and the limo's tinted glass slid down, unveiling the passing parade of ordinary, hard-working people— street vendors, motorcycle-taxi riders, school kids, the young, the old…the innocent.

He turned back to Daeng. She looked lovely in a simple cotton dress, her long black hair tied back from her face. He reached over and took her hand. She was surprised by the simple act of intimacy.

Leave the country. Flee the scene.

He heard the words over and over in his head. Upon arriving home, he took the longest, best shower of his life. Daeng threw his week-old clothes in the trash, and he climbed into the luxurious satin sheets of his own bed.

But the lawyer's words haunted him. He had his passport, and he could pack his important belongings and be at the airport in a matter of hours. It would be the sensible thing to do. It would save his life. It was what he *should* do.

16
―――――――

Jonathan Peyton sat on the leather sofa in Martin's living room. Martin stood at the sliding doors to the terrace, watching the sunset. Silence hung in the room.

Jonathan broke it. "Are you ready to tell me now?"

Martin didn't reply. Instead he moved to a bookcase where an eclectic collection of his artifacts were on display: Noh masks from Japan, carved aboriginal sun lizards, wooden Maori tattoo needles and mallet, tribal masks from Papua New Guinea, Balinese shadow puppets. The legacy of a life wandering the globe.

He picked up a pure white Hopi *kachina* doll and studied it. "The Hopi believe in shape shifting. 'Skinwalking' they call it." The doll was a warrior with a wolf's head. "A man takes the form of an animal. Do you believe in that, Mr. Peyton?"

"I believe in vampires, Martin. I've seen them."

"'Them?' You've seen more than one?"

Frustrated, Jonathan replied with an edge to his voice, "No. Just one... Come on, man. Talk to me."

Daeng watched them from the kitchen. She was separating a large pile of green peas from their long pods, but her eyes were on Martin.

Martin wandered the room, eyeing his collection of books and artifacts as if for the first time.

"Look. What I've said is true. The same beast that killed my wife is here, killing and feeding. It's time to stop him."

Martin turned to Jonathan. "You think you can stop him?"

Jonathan stood and moved next to Martin. "Yes, I can kill him."

Martin said nothing for a few moments, then turned back to his

collection. "I can't help you." He went to the front door and opened it. "I'm sorry."

Daeng watched as Jonathan left. Martin shut the door behind him and then shuffled down the hall to the bedroom.

———

It had been three hours since Jonathan left, and Daeng hadn't heard a sound from Martin. She entered the bedroom and put a glass of red wine down on the teak bedside table.

Martin lay there wearing a pair of mini-headphones connected to a CD Walkman. Daeng sat beside him, took one of the earpieces, and put it in her ear. Philip Catherine's flamenco guitar solo on "Sad Walk" came through the headset.

"That's nice."

Martin smiled. "Dig this." He put the other earphone in for her, and a sensuous trumpet came in.

"Who's that?"

"Chet Baker."

She listened to the gorgeous interplay between guitar and horn. "Beautiful."

After a few minutes, she took out the earphones and laid them on the pillow. "What's going on, Martin?"

He looked at her. She was beautiful. A beautiful woman he'd neglected. A part of his life that he almost let slip away.

He was a mortal and he needed her. He reached out to her.

She hesitated and then fell into his arms.

They made love, slowly, passionately. Martin was re-born.

He'd never thought of himself as being particularly brave. He felt he was honorable. He felt he was trustworthy. He felt he knew right from wrong. Of course, he realized, that was before he met Ramonne. Now he realized what a fool he'd been. And he knew that his path could no longer be dictated by what he *should* do. He knew what he *must* do.

17

Martin was up with the sun, feeling that he wanted to never miss another dawn again. He sat on his balcony and ate a huge breakfast as the city came to life.

He arrived at Jonathan Peyton's hotel before 8:00 a.m. The neatly appointed business inn was on a small *soi* off Silom Road, ironically, only a five-minute walk from the Hernando Cemetery. Coincidence? No, Martin decided. Jonathan planned his moves very carefully.

He was shown into the sunlit coffee shop where Jonathan was just finishing his breakfast. He looked pale, his eyes were bloodshot, and he had a hard time steadying his cup.

"My God, what's happened to you?"

"Let's go to my room, shall we?" Jonathan signed his check and led the way across the small lobby and up to the seventh floor.

The room was pleasantly appointed. It had a polished teak floor, solid Chinese furniture, and soft recessed lighting that spot-lit a couple of tasteful prints of tropical scenery. The bed's headboard was of thick, varnished bamboo, the bedspread silk and folded at the foot of the bed.

Jonathan went into the marble and granite bathroom. He

didn't close the door, and Martin couldn't help watching him from across the room. What he saw shocked him.

"What are you doing, man?" Martin stood in the open doorway.

Jonathan had a hypodermic, and was injecting his forearm.

Spread out on the stone washstand in front of him was a virtual pharmacy: pill bottles of all sizes and shapes, all sporting typed prescriptions with an Illinois Rx logo.

He finished his injection and placed the needle on a towel.

He held a cotton swab to the puncture, and bent his arm. "Sorry. I usually get all of this done before I begin my day. But, since you indicated that you hadn't been honest with me, I thought it time that I was honest with you." He swept his hand over the cornucopia of pills. "This keeps me alive."

Martin looked at the labels. Immune boosters, protease inhibitors, antiviral medications, and a multitude of vitamin supplements. Very quietly Martin said the dreaded word: "AIDS?"

"That's what the doctors think. They've diagnosed me as HIV positive, but I know different. *He* did this to me."

"The virus appeared within weeks of his attack. Showed up in a routine physical. My triglycerides were high, blood pressure was through the roof, and the white blood count was way off. And yet, I felt great. Emotionally, mentally, of course, I was a wreck. But I looked and felt wonderful. My receding hairline fully restored itself, I lost a paunch I'd been burdened with for ten years. I never needed sleep. I felt *superhuman*."

He started to open the bottles and lay the multi-colored pills in a small tray. "That lasted six months. I got the HIV diagnosis at about that time. I thought they were insane. I'd never, *never* felt stronger in my life." He started to down the pills. "And then the decline started. Now, this..." He indicated the pills and syringe. "This just gets me through the day."

Shaken, Martin went and sat by the window while Jonathan finished his cocktail. He watched the secretaries in their tight skirts, and young office workers in white shirts and loud ties buying coffee in plastic bags from the vendor across the street, before hurrying off to work.

They looked so normal.

Jonathan emerged from the bathroom and drank an orange juice from the mini bar. He had on his sunglasses and seemed much more in control of himself. He sat opposite Martin.

"I have symptoms similar to AIDS—general weakness, fatigue, etcetera. But I'm also developing an acute aversion to sunlight." He looked out the window. "I cover myself in sun block to go out now, even if it's raining."

Martin turned from the window. "I know your vampire."

He paused while Jonathan sat down.

"His name is Ramonne Delacroix."

Jonathan stared at Martin. "I have to destroy him. Destroy him before he destroys me."

"How? I mean *how* do you destroy a vampire? Do you really know?"

"Yes. I *think* I do." He went to a drawer and took out a file folder. Inside were various documents—interviews, book summaries; some taken from the Internet, some Xeroxed—all heavily marked with a yellow highlighter. All about vampires.

"As I told you, I've been obsessed with this since it happened."

Martin leafed through the papers.

"They exist, Martin. You and I know they do. They've been around for centuries. Look." He had copied documents tracing them throughout the world. "Europe, the Middle East, America, and here in Asia. I found mention of a powerful Chinese vampire in Yunnan province that was driven south in the sixteenth century."

Martin looked at the article.

"*He* could be the same one who found his way to Angkor, the one that transformed Ramonne."

Jonathan looked up. "You know his history?"

"Some of it, yes."

Jonathan ran his hand through his hair as he absorbed this fact. He shook his head.

"Anything else?" Martin handed the documents back.

"Nothing; nothing that's been published with any authenticity within a hundred years. The modern world seems to have destroyed them—innocently as it were, without ever acknowledging their existence—through simple progress. Nothing has any value any more. Everything old is plowed under and the new world rises upon its ashes. They've been driven, literally, into the light by the spread of civilization.

"Ramonne is one of very few in the world. They live in places, like Bangkok, where civilization hasn't quite caught up. Where there are still alleys to prowl and victims who won't be missed. They are *shadow people*. They live invisible, anonymous lives. They are masters at blending in. They go about their ghastly business undetected, unnoticed."

"Do you believe this stuff?" Martin asked.

"Most of it's rubbish, I admit. But some, especially this..." He indicated a stapled, ten-page transcription of a meeting between himself and a Professor Gerhardt Kaestle. It was dated just two months before, and had taken place in Professor Kaestle's office in Manhattan. "*This* I believe."

"Who is this Dr. Kaestle?"

"Entomologist. World renowned. He specializes in mosquitoes, malaria, and dengue fever. Vampire research is his hobby. He's never seen a vampire, mind you, or a vampire victim." Jonathan smiled. "That is until he met me...

"Needless to say he was spellbound by my tale. He ran another series of tests, and like the others, he concurred that my symptoms were consistent with HIV infection. But, unlike all the others, he proposed a different cure."

Martin read:

Once a victim is bitten and not killed, they will eventually develop a blood disorder. A virus. Initially the victim will acquire great strength, but this will diminish with time. Drugs will be useful in keeping the virus at bay, but will not cure the victim. The virus is telegenetic. Kill the source of origin, you kill the strain.

Again Martin asked, "But how?"

Jonathan turned a page and pointed to two highlighted paragraphs:

A vampire can be destroyed in several ways, depending on their age and strength. A 'young' vampire (a vampire for less than seventy years; their mortal age does not count) may be killed by fire. They (the young) may also be killed by direct, prolonged exposure to sunlight. Decapitation and complete destruction of the head will also kill them.

The older and more powerful a vampire becomes, the more difficult they are to eliminate. The use of fire is no longer an option. Prolonged exposure to the sun and decapitation are the only known methods but —and this is of utmost importance— an 'older' vampire, the truly 'forsaken,' can only be destroyed on hallowed ground.

Martin put the paper down. "What about the old stake through the heart?"

"Nonsense. So is garlic, the fear of crosses, and mirrors. Bram Stoker's *Dracula* is fiction. Our vampire is very real. Now, Martin. Tell me about him."

———

Martin told Jonathan about Ramonne Delacroix. He told him everything. The moment he first appeared, drinking blood from his hapless bodyguard's severed head. That first intoxicating, bloody, erotic night together, culminating in his near-death and the saving of his own skin through the mention of his considerable fortune. The depletion of his bank account. Their nightly forays. The sex, the transgressions, the opening of doors both physical and metaphysical. The conjuring of historical grandeur that was Ramonne's gift as narrator. And ultimately, his now unimaginable decision to cross over and become one of them himself.

Lastly he told of Ramonne's betrayal of his misguided trust, the brutal murder, and the collusion with the police that landed him in jail.

Jonathan sat silent throughout the tale until it was obvious that

Martin was finished.

"My God, man. Why didn't you tell me before?"

"I was under his spell. It took a week in a stinking jail to make me finally realize it."

"I've wasted two weeks, Martin. *Two fucking weeks.*" Jonathan was livid, and he slammed his fist on the table. "If you'd just been honest with me, it'd be over now."

"I'm sorry. I truly am. But look...if it wasn't for me, you'd never find him."

"I *haven't found* him yet. I've been so goddamned close. I've been clutching at straws, looking for clues while you were with him. Jesus!" He jumped to his feet and began pacing.

"We'll find him," Martin said.

"Do you know where he sleeps?"

"No. That he never revealed. But he has patterns he follows. He has places he goes."

"Then we'll search for him. Tonight."

"Jonathan, remember how dangerous he is. If he sees us first, we're dead."

"I know. We need a plan."

18

Ramonne turned the girl over and inserted himself in her rear-end. Nok shuddered, but offered no protest. Of course not. She was from the other side of the yellow line. The second girl, Porn, only took it straight. Ramonne pulled her delicious little cunt to him and licked and sucked while he hammered at the girl beneath him. Fortunately for both girls, he had fed within the last 24 hours and was only interested in sex.

He maintained this performance for a full hour until finally, the girls were completely spent, and he willed himself to a glorious voluminous climax. He had paid extra to go "bareback." *Why would I need a rubber?*

The Gardens of Babylon was a notorious sex parlor. To those who'd not visited before, its German owner, Fritz, specified quite clearly "Zat zis club is for fucking. Not for drinking. You just vant drinking, you get lost."

Located on a small *soi* off Sukhumvit's eastern reaches, it was completely nondescript outside. Inside, its lobby was circular, with a small bar, a staircase, and a yellow line. On each side of the yellow line sat about twenty very pretty girls in evening gowns. The girls on the right only 'took it in front.' While to the left…well they took it 'front and back.' Fritz was proud that you could do anything to his girls, just "Don't shit on zem. However, zey can shit on you."

Fritz encouraged his patrons to take the girls in pairs, and once the choice was made, they accompanied the client to one of forty rooms that occupied the next three floors.

Ramonne was a regular. He was actually quite pleased that he was able to control his forays enough so that he *was* welcome back at certain places. Satan knows there were enough places he wasn't welcome at. Hundreds at least. The countless times when he'd been with a whore in a short-time hotel, and he just couldn't help himself. He just *had* to kill the fucking bitch. Slit her open. Drain her dry.

He looked at the two little hookers next to him in the bed. Sweat and semen matted in their hair, nasty scratches on their backs and thighs. *I'll tip extra; who cares? They're young. They'll heal.*

They huddled together, looking wide-eyed at him. "Shower?" Nok finally had the courage to say.

Ramonne nodded and the two girls scrambled into the bathroom, clutching their towels modestly, and locking the door.

He smiled and figured what the fuck. The night was young. He'd fuck and suck them both for another hour when they got out of the bathroom.

He leaned back and listened to the shower, letting a deluge of aquatic memories pass randomly by. He settled on Lake Victoria. Zebras, wildebeest, gazelles grazing... He saw Henri Mouhot sketching madly. It was their first expedition together. They were impossibly young. They'd never been out of Isle de France and here they were documenting wildlife in the African bush. Ramonne breathed in the heady tropical air. Cranes rose in a giant flock from the lake, crossing the magnificent red orb of the sun as it set behind the water.

The sun. The fucking sun! Oh, how he missed the sun.

Red tears fell from Ramonne's eyes and stained his cheeks as he allowed himself to wallow again—just like the other thousands of times—in the memory of a sunset.

He reached under the bed and pulled out the third bottle of Pommard from his bag. He had no patience for the corkscrew Fritz had so obligingly provided. He shoved the cork into the bottle and poured the wine down his throat. In one long steady gulp, Ramonne finished half the bottle. He set it on the bedside table and looked to the bathroom. The locked door offended him. The sound of the shower offended him

As he approached the door, he imagined how much of Martin's money Herr Fritz would get from him tonight.

Oh, how he missed Martin.

Ramonne remembered first taking Martin here to the Gardens. He could gain entry anywhere, but those places he was barred from, he voluntarily chose to stay away from to avoid problems with the police. Even the royal palace wasn't off-limits to him. He'd been there countless times. Ramonne had now been a resident of the realm for so long, that just as a Thai would defend his king to his death, he too loved the monarch; felt protective of him. This was how he justified his presence in the hallowed halls. He listened to the thoughts of the guests at banquets and other functions of state that he chose to attend. Satan forbid he heard of treachery. That was certain to land the transgressor on his menu, and in the past fifty years, he liked to say, he had dined well as a result of his attendance at the palace.

But the Gardens of Babylon was at the opposite end of his social spectrum. He'd taken Martin here on numerous occasions, though how much Martin would remember, he wasn't sure.

He, of course, remembered everything!

He remembered Martin's penchant for tall girls. Ramonne had chided him on his short stature, and that this must be a mommy complex. He remembered Martin's own amazement at his second climax in a single hour. Ramonne was quite amused at that, and soon willed Martin to finish again and again, until he begged a return to normalcy.

But Martin had *something*…something that Ramonne desperately missed. A certain *joie de vivre*. Ramonne reconsidered that. *Of course he had a* joie de vivre. *He was still alive, wasn't he?*

But with Martin in tow, he could recapture his life. His mortal as well as his immortal life, and re-live it as a blessing… instead of a curse.

He sat down again. *Perhaps I should visit him.* Entering Bangrak Police Station and slipping down to the holding cells would be a simple matter. For a moment Ramonne felt a pang of guilt. *Fucking Boonsong. He makes* me *cross the yellow line. There will be a reckoning someday. This I swear.*

Yes. He *would* visit Martin. Maybe even grant his wish.

Make him a vampire.

Ramonne lurched to his feet and in one swift motion, ripped the bathroom door from its hinges and flung it across the room.

"Ahhh. My darlings. I've been waiting for you…"

———

The vampire dressed in solitude. The girls were gone now. Three hours of non-stop sex had pushed them to the brink, and they finally put modesty aside and fled naked, terrified into the hall. As Ramonne suspected, a security guard rapped sharply on the door within minutes of their departure. His terse, "Everything all right, sir?" was soon changed to *"Mai pen rai. Khawp khun khrap,"* by the simple introduction of a 1,000-baht note into his sweaty palm.

Ramonne headed for the stairs, his hand curled around a thick wad of cash he was prepared to hand to Fritz when the proprietor made his inevitable protests about his girls, their condition, the overtime, the room, its condition…

That was when he saw *them*.

19

Martin took Jonathan on a tour. Sanam Luang, Brown Sugar, the Regent, the Erawan, Patpong, Nana, everywhere he could think of that the vampire had taken *him*.

They rode boats, *tuk-tuks*, taxis, and the skytrain for endless hours, and it became apparent to Martin that when he and Ramonne had traveled, they moved without effort from one point to the next. But now he was reminded of the reality of Bangkok's infamous gridlock.

Three nights stretched into four, then five. At 1:00 a.m. on the fifth night, they walked into the Gardens of Babylon.

Fritz looked up from his crossword. After almost half a lifetime of speaking English—albeit imperfectly—and living in the City of Angels for what seemed like longer, he had still never completed the *Bangkok Times'* easy puzzle. "*Guten abend*, boys. How are you zis fine night? What iss ze other word for ze young cat. Six letters. I can only think of 'pussy.'"

"Kitten," Martin said.

"Ahh. Yes, yes. 'Kitten.' *Danke*." He filled in the spaces, then looked at his watch. "It iss a little late already, boys. Best to start ze fucking, no? Ze kittens are waiting, ha ha!"

Martin asked if Fritz had seen his friend tonight?

"Yes, yes. He iss here. Ze noise he iss making…!" Fritz rolled his eyes to the ceiling. "It iss good thing he's zuch a good tipper."

Good at tipping with my *money.* "Is it possible to get a room next to his?"

Fritz frowned and looked suspiciously at Martin and Jonathan. "For ze two of you?"

Martin quickly picked up on Fritz's concern. "With two girls, of course."

"Of course." Fritz smiled. "Only *two* girls?"

Martin shrugged. "We're a bit knackered. Two will be fine."

"Choose, choose." Fritz indicated the divided highway, and the girls primped and posed. Martin quickly grabbed the first two to the right, Ying and Ping.

Fritz handed him a key—"For you, room 319. Your friend iss in 320. Enjoy"—then went back to his crossword.

Upstairs, Martin was disappointed to see that 319 was, in fact, not next to 320, but across from it, just a little further down the corridor.

"Shit." He knew that there were balconies on the front of the building—the *even* side he realized—and that it would be easy to gain access from one balcony to the next.

The girls both jumped as a piercing scream was heard from Ramonne's room, followed quickly by a loud slap and the vampire's chilling laugh.

Martin unlocked the door to their room and hustled the girls inside. Ping pointed to the bathroom door and said, "Shower first." Which was exactly what Martin had hoped.

Yes. Yes. By all means…a nice long shower.

"In fact," he told them, "lock the door and stay in there for the next hour. Okay?"

He reached for his billfold and handed each of them 5,000 baht.

Their eyes grew wide as saucers. For that amount they'd do anything—all night long.

Ying muttered something and giggled as she and Ping closed the bathroom door.

As soon as the girls were out of the way, Jonathan went to work. He picked up the leather case he'd hauled all over Bangkok for the last five nights, and opened it on the bed. He had not been idle in his two weeks in town. Professor Kaestle had provided him with a shopping list, and though all of the items would be considered illegal, they were readily attainable on Wang Burapa Road, Bangkok's black-market arms depot.

He extracted two rifle stocks from the foam padding, and two matching short barrels. He snapped each barrel onto its stock, and locked it in place with a twist. The barrels were actually twin tubes, giving the gun the appearance of a very short, double-barreled shotgun. He laid the matching weapons on the bedspread.

In the top of the case was a small compartment from which Jonathan took out four metal cylinders that looked like expensive Churchill cigars. He laid them beside the two guns on the bed, and twisted two open. Inside were large darts. They had bright-red plumage, and a fat barrel tapering to a needle-sharp point.

Jonathan unhinged one of the double-barreled guns and carefully slid in the two darts, snapping the barrels back in place with a resounding *kachunk*! He laid it down and cautiously performed the same procedure on the other gun.

"Ketamine. A hundred ccs in each hypodermic dart," Jonathan had already explained when he'd first showed Martin the guns at his hotel. "Enough to drop a bull elephant in its tracks."

"But how will this stop *him*? You told me yourself that you saw bullets pass right through, without fazing him."

"That's right. The bullets passed through. That's *exactly* the difference. The ketamine will go straight into his blood system. It *will* stop him. That I'm sure of. But for how long…?" He had shrugged. "That's anyone's guess."

But long enough, he hoped, to drag the vampire to hallowed ground and decapitate him.

"And how do we do *that*?" Martin really didn't want to know.

"With this." Jonathan had then opened his closet and pulled out a golf bag. Parting the clubs, he took a long leather case from the middle.

Inside was a Remington 12-gauge shotgun. He pumped it once, chambering a round, and pointed it at the window. "Boom." He mimed pulling the trigger. "Decapitated and destroyed in one swift move." He'd extracted the round and zippered the gun back into its case.

"How the fuck do you know any of this will work?"

"I don't. But Martin, what are my options?"

They crouched in the dark outside their door and waited. Each had a double-barreled gun, cocked and ready. Martin wasn't sure of his ability to do this, as guns were not something he was familiar with. In fact, outside of a beloved Daisy Red Ryder BB gun he had as a boy, this was the first gun he'd held in thirty years.

"Aim low," Jonathan advised him.

The girls had left room 320. They'd fled the scene about ten minutes earlier. They'd been followed shortly by a security guard who took a token payment and went away satisfied that all was well in the Gardens of Babylon.

Now Ramonne was alone. They could hear him humming. A Beethoven sonata. They assumed he was dressing.

They sat in their positions and waited…

Shortly before 2:00 a.m. the door opened. Ramonne stepped into the hall, and started for the stairs when his vampire radar went off.

He swung upon them.

"Martin!" He hissed and began to move toward them, just as Jonathan fired. The dart hit him square in the heart, and he stopped, curious as to what was sticking in his chest. He moved to pull the missile out when Jonathan fired again. The second struck him in the right shoulder. He whipped his head toward Jonathan and leapt.

"Martin! Fire! Shoot—"

Ramonne was right upon Jonathan, ripping the weapon from his hands. As he flung it aside, Martin fired. The dart struck the vampire in the back, almost dead center. This one he tried to reach, but could not. He growled, bared his fangs, and bent over Jonathan, who locked his arms in an attempt to defend himself.

"Martin!" he screamed.

Martin fired again, this time hitting the vampire in the leg.

Four hundred ccs of ketamine finally went to work. Ramonne relaxed his grip, turning to Martin with a look of utter astonishment before he collapsed.

———

Two in the morning and Silom Road was gridlocked.

"Straight on," Martin screamed at the taxi driver, imploring him not to enter Silom, which was a sea of tail-lights for the next two miles. But grinning maniacally and repeating "Thissaway, thissaway," the cabbie did just what Martin feared. And locked them into the traffic jam.

"Oh, for Christ's sake!" Martin sagged in the seat. Ramonne's head was on Jonathan's shoulder, and it bobbed like a Kewpie doll when the car came to a halt.

"Out, out," Jonathan yelled. He unlatched his door and hoisted Ramonne to his feet, the vampire looking for all the world like a drunken sailor.

Martin fished in his pocket for some money, which he threw at the still grinning driver. As he got out, he left both the passenger door and the rear door wide open, so the cabbie would have to get out and close them himself.

Jonathan surveyed the gridlocked landscape. "Which way?"

"There." Martin pointed across four lanes of stationary traffic on Rama IV. "We head for Sathorn Road. It's our only hope." He took hold of Ramonne's other side and they dragged the hapless vampire through the impromptu parking lot.

When at last they reached the north side of the road, they flagged down another cab, and pushing Ramonne ahead of them, climbed in. Martin gave directions, and the taxi sped off, unimpeded.

They moved down Sathorn Road and turned right under the skytrain onto the new road with the unpronounceable name. The traffic was lighter here, and it was just minutes before they made a left back into Silom nearer their destination, having successfully avoided the gridlock. The cab crept to the next block.

Ramonne started to stir. Martin looked nervously to Jonathan.

"Stop," Jonathan called out, and the cab pulled to the curb. They hauled Ramonne with them as they staggered the last two blocks to Hernando Cemetery.

Outside the iron gates, Jonathan leaned the now recovering vampire onto Martin, while he took a small spray can from his pocket.

"Jesus. He's waking up. Hurry." Martin flinched as Ramonne put his arm around his shoulder and stroked his hair.

Jonathan attacked the rusty padlock with the nitroglycerin spray. The metal turned silver and then frosty white. He bent down and picked up a broken chunk of pavement, slamming it into the lock, which broke clean in half. He pushed the gate, and it creaked and groaned inward.

Hallowed ground.

They dragged Ramonne inside and laid him on a tomb in

the open graveyard. His head lolled from side to side, recovering.

"The gun! Get the gun!" Martin yelled.

Jonathan went to the Hernando Mausoleum, and threw open the gate that they both knew was never locked. He dashed inside, and in a moment reappeared in the doorway.

"It's not here!"

"Of course it is. I saw you put it in there earlier. Maybe it fell down."

Martin ran into the tomb. He took the flashlight from Jonathan and swung it wildly about. There was little to see. A large marble tomb in the center, and two huge flower urns that earlier had seemed the perfect hiding place for a Remington shotgun.

Outside they heard Ramonne moan.

"Jesus. It's *got* to be here." Martin pushed the urn, and it shattered on the cold stone floor. It was empty.

"Martin." Jonathan stood in the open doorway, looking out at the cemetery.

"What? Did you find it?"

"I found it." Jonathan raised his empty hands over his head. He stared straight ahead.

"Yudie?" Martin couldn't believe his eyes.

The old woman stood next to the tomb, the shotgun cradled onto the strut of a tombstone cross to steady her aim.

She had been targeting Jonathan, but now she swung it on Martin. "Why did you bring your gun into my garden? Why won't you ever leave me alone?" Her ancient eyes stared into Martin's very soul.

"Khun Yudie, I mean you no harm."

Next to Yudie, Ramonne opened his eyes.

"Yudie. Give me the gun," Martin pleaded. "Now, please."

"So much trouble here after you came. I tried not to pay attention, but how can I look away? You brought the police. They told me they will shut my garden down. They will move my flowers. All because of you." Her finger was on the trigger.

"Yudie. It's not I who desecrates your garden. It's him. *He* causes the trouble. *He* brought the police."

Next to her, Ramonne sat up. He looked from Martin to Jonathan and smiled. "Hello, Martin. I see my friend has returned to Siam."

"Yudie! For God's sake shoot him."

Ramonne turned to the old woman. The gun quivered in her grasp and he smiled. "Mother," he said. "Put down the gun."

Yudie's eyes widened as she slowly did as he commanded. As the shotgun lifted off the cross, the weight was too much for her, and it clattered to the ground.

"Jadesada?" Yudie's eyes watered as she looked at Ramonne.

"Yes, Mother." He motioned her to him.

She stumbled to him, seeing not Ramonne but her young son. He embraced her and she sobbed on his shoulder. He stroked the gray hair on her old head, and then turned to Jonathan with a look so malevolent, it sent a cold shock through his veins.

His eyes on Jonathan, Ramonne kissed Yudie's head and then twisted it sharply until the inevitable *crack*!

"No!" Martin screamed.

Without taking his eyes off Jonathan, Ramonne let Yudie slither to the ground.

Jonathan leapt for the gun. He hit the ground hard, grabbed the weapon, and rolled onto his side. Ramonne rose to his feet and made an impossible jump to the top of the mausoleum. Jonathan aimed and fired, the shotgun blast deafening in the night calm as it bounced off the stone walls.

It was all for naught. Ramonne was gone even before Jonathan pulled the trigger.

Jonathan had known from the outset that if he didn't destroy Ramonne when he was comatose, he didn't stand a chance.

They went to the old woman's shack and found the case for the gun. Jonathan hoisted it over his shoulder, shut the gate to the cemetery, and they silently blended into the thinning crowd on Silom.

Martin recited a childhood prayer for Yudie, sure that now Lord, all her troubles be over.

He was just as sure that he had caused her death. Another death.

20

———————

The light played across the sunflowers the way Beethoven's notes washed over his finely attuned ears. Music and art, his mother had taught him, go hand in glove.

The little Van Gogh was totally unknown, but oh, how Ramonne treasured it. Gently he brushed his finger over the crusts of paint, savoring their peaks and valleys. He sighed and sat back down in the tattered Louis XIV armchair.

His surroundings reflected who he was. Two centuries of life were arranged in this windowless catacomb beneath the Lumpini Stadium. Above him, every night, as in a Roman arena, the battle was fought. Sometimes, when it pleased him, he joined the fray— shouting, cursing, and gambling along with the frenetic crowd—as the atonal band played their soundtrack to the wiry little warriors who gave their hearts, each and every night, each and every fight.

In one corner, scores of vintage wine bottles rested in their cradles, honeycombed into the damp wall by a golden spider's web, woven to his design by a skilled craftsman.

There was a comfortable coffin in the center of the room. The lamps—wired, he was proud to say, for fifty-odd years, into the stadium's main circuit—were Tiffany. There were other fine

Louis XIV furnishings, all now sadly a little threadbare, and there were books. Hundreds of them. All first editions. Priceless. The ornate gold shelving, built at the same time as the wine cradles, dominated more than half the space.

Ramonne sipped the last of his wine and set it next to the turntable. He selected a record. *None of that CD shit.* His ears were so finely tuned that a CD was merely an offensive, acoustically flat version of what music used to be. He hadn't listened to anything recorded after 1978.

Sketches of Spain seemed borne on a warm breeze that floated from the speakers, and he wanted to fly. He *could* fly…at least he could leap great distances in the blink of an eye. But he was at home now, and he resisted the urge.

He picked up a silver-framed daguerreotype of a young woman, softly caressing it before setting it back on the mantle. Then he opened the lid to his coffin, fluffed up the pillow, and settled into its satin interior.

His thoughts drifted unchecked to Martin. *Ah. Martin. Martin. What is it you want now?*

Martin. His charge. How did it all go so wrong? How was it that now…now, Martin wanted to kill him.

He'd offered Martin eternal life. The gift.

The greatest gift that he could give.

Yeah, okay, so that cocksucker Boonsong forced me to fuck it all up and turn Martin into a victim for the sake of drawing the considerable fucking heat off my fucking back. So what? Nobody got hurt, did they?

And he had planned to fix it. He was going to spring Martin. Really turn him into a vampire.

But no! Martin had to get all involved with that American.

Fucking pansy. Wife told me she loved my tongue as I sucked the life out of her!

He thought of the woman. When he first saw her. He was in the bar of their hotel. High on a cliff overlooking Pattaya Bay…

Odd choice it was for a vampire, a beachside resort. However, it was but a two-hour drive from Bangkok. A lovely full moon. Ramonne had insisted upon a convertible, and he had the driver throw the top back. He howled with delight as the night air washed through his flowing hair.

Pattaya was unique in the world of beachside resorts in that it was famous for its nightlife—much more than for its dirty beaches and polluted water—boasting miles and miles of bars, wall to wall whores, lovely dark stretches where the road from the seafront joined the highway to Jomtien and points south. He would wait in the bushes for a victim to approach…leaping out as a bike rider leaned into the curve. Then drain the carcass and place it alongside the wrecked machine. Another motorbike death.

There were the pedophiles, whose idea of heaven on earth was trolling the beaches for young boys and girls. Ramonne abhorred those who preyed on children. He'd stalk the degenerates as they pursued their little victims, taking them viciously, ripping their throats open and reveling in their gurgles of death.

It was a wonderful vacation. His bloodlust had been almost out of control, and the police were complaining about the number and frequency of the bodies they were required to dispose of. So he'd gone off to make himself scarce for a while.

He had recently made a new acquaintance in Bangkok, an investment broker; Belgian, a young upstart, constantly talking a language that Ramonne could barely make heads or tails of. It was English, yes—that, the vampire understood perfectly—but it was punctuated with investment gibberish and finance babble: "angel funding," "upsides, downsides." *Etceteras, etceteras…* It drove Ramonne nuts, the little prat's posturing and proselytizing over long, expensive dinners—at which Ramonne drank bottle after bottle of red wine, and watched him eat. And then Ramonne would pay the bill.

But he had needed the cunt to broker a deal for him in regards to his trust fund. The minute that was concluded, Ramonne had ripped his head off, drunk his blood, and eaten his brain. A special occasion.

In going through the late investment banker's effects, Ramonne came across a key and directions to a quiet bungalow in Pattaya. Thus the vampire's holiday plans were finalized.

The house sat alone at the end of a cul-de-sac, overlooking the sea. Across a small canyon was the Royal Cliff Hotel, aglow in golden lamplight. Ramonne was drawn to the warm lights, and would begin most evenings with a drink in the bar, as the guests strolled the grounds or relaxed, lingering over their dinners. What was a nightcap for most, was a wake-up tonic for Ramonne.

He'd been there for three nights when she walked in. Her long, tousled auburn hair radiated with the light of the lamp directly behind her. It practically threw off sparks. She had a fine, smooth neck, with a single strand of white pearls resting against warm skin kissed by the tropical sun. She wore a light-peach gown that left her shoulders bare and exposed the tops of her perfect breasts. An angel.

The young man next to her held her hand lightly, their fingers intertwined. Her thumb kept gliding along the smooth gold band he wore. She was so in love. Newlyweds. As they passed his table, Ramonne sniffed the air and drew in a long, lingering taste of her. Her perfume, her sweat, her essence. She had recently made love. *They* had made love. Already Ramonne despised the young man.

They sat at the bar, laughing. She leaned in and nuzzled the man's neck, then gently tugged on his earlobe with her perfect teeth. They drank vodka martinis…*Americans*…and shared their olives. She shifted to sit more comfortably on the barstool, and Ramonne glimpsed her inner thigh… *My destination.* She smoothed out the gown and turned away from the vampire's gaze.

He had to have her.

They stayed in the bar for another drink, then left.

Ramonne signaled for his check, paid it quickly, and walked out to the garden.

They were there. Kissing in the moon's falling beams. Ramonne stayed in the shadows, wanting to rush the young man, rip out his foolish heart, and spirit her away.

Soon they wandered on down the path and up the outside stairs to a private villa. Ramonne watched the light turn on, and he moved to the base of the stairs. A stately banyan tree stood alongside, and Ramonne climbed to a wide branch outside what proved to be their bedroom window. There he watched as the two mortals made love.

They were slow, tender; the man treating her with a reverence that Ramonne had forgotten. He watched as they intertwined, he always gentle, she softly moaning, smiling in ecstasy as she held him to her. They were as one.

Ramonne watched and remembered *that* kind of love. Remembered back 150 years. Remembered the girl…Giselle… that he'd left at the dock in Marseilles. Remembered the nights they'd spent together. Remembered the promises. Promises stolen by a vampire in a stone temple concealed by jungle.

He was so young. The chill wind blew off the water in the harbor at Marseilles, causing the breath of the dock workers to float above their heads like tiny clouds. The good ship *Christienne* was being loaded with the last of its cargo. Most hands were already on board. But a man and a woman on the dock were lost in an eternal embrace.

Ramonne gazed into the beautiful cerulean pools of Giselle's eyes. Lord, how he loved that woman.

Against his family's wishes, he had pursued his passion for art. He'd been a student at the Academie d'Lyons when they'd met. She was 14, a child. Ramonne's taste for café au lait and fresh croissants led him to her mother's *boulangerie* each morning. He would sit in the shop and finish the assignments that were heaped, it seemed, by the pound upon the freshman students.

Each time she refilled his cup, Giselle would eye the young man's life drawings, anatomy sketches, still lifes, and free-form sketches. By his senior year, she shared his one-room studio overlooking the harbor, and was the subject of his painting. Canvases reflected her every mood—clothed and unclothed. They were wed shortly after he graduated.

But an artist's life is one of uncertainty. Ramonne struggled — too proud to ask his father for money—and they existed on her paltry income for years. Not that life was other than bitter-sweet, but Ramonne wanted so much for his love.

But then there was the chance encounter with Henri Mouhot, and all changed. The explorer happened into the café, and expressed his appreciation of Ramonne's work, which adorned the walls. Impressed with the young man's style and spirit, Mouhot offered him a position. Soon, as Mouhot's *chargé d'affaires*, Ramonne was able to give Giselle a taste of the life he desired for her. Nights at the opera, weekends in Avignon, jewelry…things she'd never known.

And then that chill, February day when they said goodbye at the dock, Mouhot watching from aboard the ship. The magnificent clipper would carry them around the world—a year's journey or more.

Sweet Giselle would wait. Would be there upon his return. She slipped from his embrace and handed him a packet. He unfolded the tissue wrapping to find a silver pocket watch. She wound it for him and he put it into his breast pocket.

He held and kissed her…for the last time. Then climbed the gangplank and watched her beautiful figure become reduced to a speck.

She was gone. Forever.

———

Ramonne watched the mortals as red tears slipped down his face. He no longer wanted to devour her. He wanted to love her.

For three more nights he watched them. Discreetly. They had a routine. A late dinner in the hotel restaurant, martinis in the bar, walking, and making love. After, they would sleep, and Ramonne would slip into the night to feed.

The next night, Ramonne spent an hour in the bath. He had put a lavender conditioner on his hair, and combed it back with a trendy gel substance he'd found in the cottage. He then sat in the restaurant wearing his finest suit, with his wine and a tureen of soup. Beef broth was one of the few mortal foods he could tolerate. He'd fed early, chancing the crowds and authorities. His bloodlust was in check.

And he waited.

After an hour and one bottle of Brouilly, she appeared. They'd been shopping, and tonight she wore a simple white blouse, which tied across one shoulder, and a shimmering silk sarong wrapped tightly around her slim waist. She had an orchid tucked in her hair, and again the pearls shone against her skin, which had obtained the deeper glow of another day in the sun. The man held her chair. Ramonne would have to remember that. Chivalry. She sat facing Ramonne.

His heart raced. This was extraordinary. He wasn't even sure his heart still beat at all, and now it was about to burst. He tried to make eye contact, but she looked only at her husband. Her lover. Oh, how he despised him.

The waiter brought a fresh bottle of wine and took away the untouched soup. Ramonne slid his chair back, making the heavy legs scrape on the floor. She looked his way. He smiled and nodded. She ignored him and looked back to her husband.

Ramonne walked to the lobby and took a mobile phone from his pocket. He detested these instruments, the constant intrusions, but he admitted that occasionally they had their uses. This one he had taken from a dead whore. He dialed the hotel number and watched as the girl at the desk answered the phone. He asked for the young man. She said, "Just a moment," and put him on hold. He threw the phone in the trash and walked back into the restaurant.

As he entered, the bellboy was leading Jonathan to the lobby. He paid no attention to Ramonne as their paths crossed.

Ramonne strode purposefully to their table. She looked up in surprise as he sat in Jonathan's recently vacated seat.

"Yes? May I help you?" she asked.

He read not a trace of fear.

"Jennifer," he spoke.

"How do you know my name?" She was curious, not shocked.

"I know everything about you. I know your favorite color… peach. The name of your cocker spaniel…Pepito. The little blue house with the white picket fence you were raised in… I know *everything*." Ramonne leaned in. He knew he had just moments. Moments to make her love him.

He willed her to. He projected the most beautiful images he could conjure. His mind spoke of a gorgeous ranch, white horses, fields of lilacs…things he knew she desired. Things he knew he could give her.

"Jennifer." He held out his hand. "Come with me."

She extended her hand. He folded her freshly painted finger-nails into his palm.

He led her outside to where the terrace opened onto the gardens, and took her down a secluded path to a wooden bench surrounded by flowers and sculptures. Life-sized couples engaged in hedonistic embraces as bougainvillea erupted around them.

He stroked her hair and looked deep into her eyes. Jennifer was intoxicated, under his spell. Beautiful clouds moved across the night sky. The flowers opened into full bloom. The statues tightened their embraces…

And Jennifer became Giselle.

Ramonne smiled.

"Who are you?" Jennifer-Giselle asked.

"Your lover," Ramonne replied. He pulled her to him and kissed her. "Oh, how I've longed for you."

For a moment she saw it all. Saw them together. Making love. It was beautiful. All she could desire.

Ramonne broke the embrace and held her at arm's length as he reached into his pocket. He took out the silver pocket watch.

"All these years, my love. I've never forgotten."

He put the watch in her hand.

She looked at it, confused. "I don't understand."

"Giselle. You…"

With the words, Giselle once again became Jennifer. The spell was broken.

"Giselle—"

"Who?" Jennifer started to stand. The flowers behind her began to wilt.

Ramonne's smile faded and he reached out to her. At his touch, she dropped the watch…and he now saw her as Jennifer.

The sky turned red and the statues were now alive. In each, the man turned from embracing his lover to sinking his teeth into her neck. The alabaster turned crimson as their passion became an orgy of bloodlust.

Jennifer shrieked and pulled her hand away. "How *dare* you?" She slapped him—hard. She was poised to strike again, but instead she got up and left.

Ramonne sat silently as the sky and the statues slowly returned to their normal poses.

———

Silently, Ramonne climbed the banyan tree, pulling himself up like a cat. He settled on a stout branch, and watched. The girl was furious. Such fire. Such superb spirit. Such passion.

Jonathan arrived and she yelled at him. He paced the room,

obviously uncertain what to do. Finally she made a decision, throwing open the closet and pulling out a leather bag. She placed it on the bed and began to fold her clothes into it. Jonathan tried to stop her, gently placing a hand on her shoulder, but she threw him off and shook her head. She continued packing.

Packing? Leaving? This Ramonne could not allow. She would not leave him. He would have her.

He stood on the branch and leapt.

They both spun at the sound of the smashing glass, and saw Ramonne. She started to scream, but the breath was knocked from her as he picked her up and slung her over his shoulder. Jonathan yelled something and reached for Ramonne, who swung his free hand backward with such fury that the blow knocked Jonathan across the room.

In a second, Ramonne was out the window, where he leapt to the ground. He stared up at the shattered window frame and saw Jonathan. Then turned and sprinted across the garden with the girl across his shoulder.

—————

It had been clumsy, his attempt at romance and seduction. Well, what could one expect after 150 years? He was a little out of practice. And besides, vampires do things differently.

He mourned her. Jennifer. He still remembered waking her — *after* he'd taken off her clothes. Vampires do things differently. And he remembered that scream! Exactly like Elsa Lancaster in that old Frankenstein movie, the one where she played the monster's bride. And the way she fought. Magnificent. He remembered how she finally succumbed, surrendering at last. He remembered her moans as he lowered his head between her legs. Finally she was *his*. She held his head and trembled. And then he remembered the moment he took her life. For he knew she would never remain his.

———

He drew the silver watch from his vest pocket, wound it—a practice he'd performed daily for a century and a half—and gently put it back. He sighed and closed the lid on his coffin. In the dark, he thought of Martin.

He actually tried to kill me. The ungrateful little prick.

21

———

Jonathan lay in the dark. Outside he heard the traffic. Outside he heard the pedestrians. Outside he heard their voices. Outside he *heard* their thoughts. Faintly...far away. He couldn't separate them. He couldn't single out an individual. But it wasn't so much a *sound* as a feeling that he'd never experienced before.

He had tried to look out the window, but now he could not abide the sunlight at all. Just a glance at the daylight seared his eyes, and he instantly closed the heavy drape and crawled back into bed.

If he turned his head from the window, the intrusive sounds faded. But now he heard the thoughts of the guests as they passed in the hall. Though faint, they were clear enough: "Oh, Christ. Not the shits again. Another day sitting on the loo. Where's that fucking key?" From his British neighbor directly adjacent. Fortunately, most guests were gone in the day, and the maids and help thought in Thai, which was gibberish to him. It didn't intrude as much on his own tortured thoughts.

What the fuck is happening?

It had been two and a half days since the botched attempt at killing the vampire. Sixty hours. He'd been unable to leave his room in that time. He'd lain in his bed in the day and sat at his window at night. He'd tried taking his medicine, but had been unable to keep anything down.

He'd had nothing to eat or drink in those sixty hours. And yet, for the first time in months, he felt his strength returning.

As darkness fell, he rose from the bed and opened the drapes. He swung the window out and breathed in the night air, overwhelmed by a potpourri of smells. Delicious aromas of the night that made him light-headed. The annoying swirl of thoughts was replaced by a sense that he could taste the air. He stretched and felt muscles in his arms and back that he had not been aware of before. He went into the bathroom and looked in the mirror. The face that stared back was almost unrecognizable. Gone was the sickly pallor, the bloodshot eyes, and matted hair. The man in the mirror seemed ten years younger and a hundred times stronger. He swept the mass of pill bottles from the granite washbasin and into the trash.

He showered, reveling in the fragrant water running over his chiseled body, and instead of toweling off, he walked naked to the window and let the warm night breeze dry him.

He'd reconstructed that night many times. And he'd looked at the small cut on his left wrist many more, willing it to disappear. But of course, it did not. It was healing. That was fine. But it was not going to disappear.

He'd been bitten. During the struggle in the hallway of the whorehouse. *Bitten.* Just a scratch, really. Nothing. It was healing fine. It had started to form a scar.

He remembered screaming to Martin to shoot as the vampire bared his fangs and loomed over him. He had held him off long enough for Martin to shoot. The vampire had turned to the shot, and in turning, his razor-sharp incisor sliced Jonathan's wrist. Jonathan recalled his horror at the moment, but in the panic that followed, it was forgotten.

Jonathan *knew* what was happening to him. Much as he wanted to deny it.

He picked up the phone and called Martin.

22

"If we act fast, before I lose my mind completely, we can use me to get to him." Jonathan spoke in an excited voice just above a whisper. "I can track him. I can lure him."

Martin had to lean closer over the din of the restaurant.

He had been relieved to get Jonathan's call. He'd tried the hotel numerous times, on each occasion being assured that Mr. Peyton was not taking any calls, and that Martin's message would be added to the small pile of notes being slipped quietly under his door. Sometimes Martin hated hotels' overprotective attitude to their guests. But he had to admit that when he was on the other side, he always used the front desk as a wall against the world.

But, Christ, they had just been at war with a vampire! It was a thought that, try as he might to express his urgency, he was unable to articulate. And so he waited.

When Jonathan did call, he sounded so calm that Martin almost didn't recognize the voice.

And now, sitting across from him in the Italian restaurant at the Erawan Hotel, he didn't recognize the face.

"Jesus, man! A few days rest has done wonders for you. You look great." Martin marveled.

When the waitress came, Jonathan ignored the menu. "Steak. Blood rare. And some wine. Red."

Martin chose a carafe of the house wine, figuring that he'd be paying. He ordered a crab salad and his usual boring glass of soda water. "With lime." For a little flavor.

"I feel…different, Martin. I'm changing. I'm becoming one of *them*."

"What? Ridiculous. Your medicine must be working is all."

"I threw it out." Jonathan unbuttoned his shirt cuff and rolled it back. "Look." He turned his hand over, and Martin saw the small scar on the inside wrist.

"Ramonne. As we struggled and you shot him with the dart."

"Jesus!" Martin stared at the wound. "It's so small. Are you sure?"

"It's the *second* bite. That's how you're turned."

Martin remembered the literature:

To 'turn' his prey into one of the forsaken, the vampire must not kill it, but must bring it to the brink of death and mix his own blood with that of the chosen one. Failing that, should the victim recover, a second bite will cause the transformation into the unholy.

"My God!" Martin realized that but for the *grace of God*, he'd be saying Jonathan's words. In his mind he gave a prayer.

"I'm not sure He hears you."

"What?"

"Your prayer. I'm not sure that *He* hears you."

"You can read my thoughts…already?"

"I can't shut it off. I read *everybody's* thoughts." He winced. "Don't envy me, Martin."

Martin was embarrassed. That was exactly what he was doing. With a shudder, he snapped out of it. "Are you sure? This could be just another phase of your illness."

"It's not. I'm not ill anymore. I've never felt stronger in my life. Look." Jonathan took the stainless-steel soup spoon and bent it in two with one hand. "And my eyes. I look down the street, and I see forever. I see *everything*."

"What will you do?"

"What I've always intended to do. Destroy Ramonne. But we must hurry. I feel the bloodlust already."

Their food arrived. Jonathan devoured the steak. Then he upended the plate and drank the red juices.

"I need another. And tell them not to cook it at all this time."

"I can't tell them that. That's barbaric."

Jonathan rolled his eyes. "Please."

"I'll have them sear the edges."

"Whatever. I'm famished. I could eat a cow."

"I'm sure you could. Maybe we should just go rent a dairy farm for a while."

Jonathan looked queerly at him.

"I'm kidding. Eat your potatoes."

"I can't. Just looking at them makes me nauseous."

"And the wine?" Martin asked.

"Bitter. Rancid. I'd have them take it back, but I've already drunk half of it."

So wine snobbery comes with the territory.

Martin placed the order and picked at his crab salad.

"We have to move swiftly. I don't know how long I'll be able to control my cravings."

"You must."

"I know that, man. But I'm afraid that saying it and doing it are going to be two entirely different matters."

They fell into silence for a while until the second steak arrived, looking like it was straight from the butcher. The waitress stood by, certain the *farang* would send it back. Martin nodded and she went away. *Farang baa* Jonathan heard her thinking while he consumed the second steak, again savoring the bloody juices.

"You won't be able to eat in public for much longer," Martin observed.

"I'm sure there are *many* things I won't be able to do soon. Public or otherwise." He wiped his smeared lips. "I can't be in the sun now—period. I tried looking out the window today, and it burned."

Martin watched as Jonathan winced, finishing off the wine.

"We must start tonight. I'm sure I can find him."

———

Having failed once, this time they knew would probably be their last chance. They also needed a driver.

After dinner, and against his better judgment, Martin got the keys from Daeng. She had scoffed at the idea: "You, driving? Hah! Where are you going? I'll drive you. I always drive you."

Martin couldn't allow that, but then Jonathan took him aside. "I've been thinking… He can't resist a helpless female. We could use a decoy."

"*Daeng*? Are you out of your fucking mind? No way!"

He grabbed Martin's arm. "Yes. I probably am 'out of my fucking mind.' Or soon will be." His grip was like a vise.

Martin pulled free. "Okay, okay. But she just drives. That way we can concentrate on finding him. She just drives. She stays in the car."

"Absolutely."

They went back into the living room, where Daeng was already waiting with her jacket. She knew the air conditioning in the car at *farang* temperature would cause her to catch a cold.

"All right. Let's do it now," Jonathan ordered.

Martin proceeded with trepidation. Daeng was just glad to get out of the house. "You're looking good, Jonathan," she said on the way to the elevator. "You been working out?"

"Yes, sort of," Jonathan hedged.

"You're smart. Martin's too fat. *Meuan muu.* And lazy. Never exercises. Just eat, eat, eat."

"Daeng, please." Martin couldn't stand the irony of her admiring a man for turning into a vampire. If she only knew.

They drove straight to Jonathan's hotel. Daeng stayed with the car while Jonathan and Martin assembled their arsenal. They came downstairs, with Martin carrying the golf bag. This caused a few odd looks, the hour approaching midnight, but hotel decorum was respected and the curious looks were quickly converted to smiles and *wais.*

They dumped the load in the trunk of the Cherokee and climbed back in.

"Where to? All-night golf range?" Daeng asked.

———

Two million baht was a lot of money in Thailand. Six years salary for most people. And when packaged in 1,000-baht notes —20,000 of them—it made a pretty thick envelope.

Ramonne felt like a fool standing in the shadows, waiting for the cunt Boonsong, outside of the Darling Massage Parlor on Soi 12. Two Mercedes, a Rolls Royce, and a Jaguar were parked next to a green cherub who pissed a continual stream into a golden koi-carp pond.

Ramonne checked his silver pocket watch. He hated waiting. He'd give him his fucking money. *But soon...oh very soon... there'll be a reckoning.*

Eventually the lieutenant-colonel emerged from the neon parlor. No brown uniform tonight. A blue shirt-jac, as they used to be called in the fifties—the last time they were in fashion —hanging outside his brown polyester sans-a-belt slacks.

Such a fashion plate. The best you'll ever look is when I cover you with your own fucking blood.

Boonsong lit a cigarette and told his driver to wait a moment while he had a smoke. He took a stroll...

"How was she?" Ramonne asked as Boonsong approached. "She was fine. A little old. I like them young, you know. Nineteen or so."

Boonsong was 45. The girl in the parlor was probably younger than his daughter. The daughter Ramonne knew was constantly on the lieutenant-colonel's mind. For she was a naughty girl. Always in the wrong place at the wrong time. Raids on bars where ecstasy was dispensed like candy. Shoot-outs between rival spoiled-brat sons of shady politicians. She was often photographed hanging onto the wrong arm. These little misdemeanors cost the colonel plenty. Money, no doubt, that Ramonne was providing.

"But, I can't complain. It costs *me* nothing." Boonsong laughed. "Just the tip of course."

Policeman's discount. Same the world over. The *gendarmes* in Marseilles got their croissants and café au lait *au gratis* Ramonne recalled. But, then again, that was 150 years ago. Never mind, he was sure it was the same and worse. As for tipping…Ramonne pictured the well-worn 100-baht note that the skin-tight cop had handed the girl.

"You have the payment?" Boonsong demanded as he stubbed out his cigarette.

"Two million baht is a lot of fucking money. Pardon my French. What makes you think I can come up with that?"

"Why…?" Boonsong drew dangerously close to the vampire. The impudence of the mortal was astounding. "Because you have to. You don't, and I crush you. I expose you. I say all the *farang's* stories are true. They will hunt you down and destroy you. It's my constant denial of your existence that keeps you in line."

Boonsong held out his hand, but Ramonne made no move. He was so close to ripping his fucking heart out.

"Oh, and by the way. We've closed up Hernando Cemetery. Permanently. It's been bought by the government. Very valuable piece of property. We'll be moving its occupants out to

Sam Phran, Nakhon Pathom province. Nice and peaceful out there."

Ramonne hissed.

Boonsong shrugged his shoulders and held out his hand.

Ramonne handed over the envelope. "A *lot* of fucking money."

"I know it's a lot of fucking money. But you have been making a lot of fucking trouble for me. Dropping bodies like flies in my district. For the last two weeks—"

"*One* you asked for," Ramonne reminded him.

"Yeah. For your little friend, Larue. This is his money isn't it?"

Ramonne shrank back. Was it possible this mortal had the gift?

"I know everything that happens in my district. I know you've been bleeding that rich little prick. *Mai pen rai.* I've got my own plans for him and his bank account. What's left of it, that is." He hefted the thick envelope, emphasizing the point. "And speaking of Mr. Larue—why didn't you just kill him when you had the chance?"

Why not indeed?

"If you want. I'll leave your district," Ramonne offered.

"Oh, please do. You're getting to be an embarrassment, to say the least. Please get out of Bangrak. Get the fuck out of Bangkok for that matter..." He tapped the vampire on the chest with the envelope. "But don't think you won't still owe me."

Ramonne made a low growl.

Boonsong held the envelope in Ramonne's face. "This will never stop. *This* keeps you alive." He turned and walked to his car.

Ramonne remained rock still and glared. He knew if he allowed himself to move a fraction of an inch, he would leap onto Boonsong and rip him to shreds.

Boonsong's driver put a small red light on top of the Mercedes and switched it on. With the light flashing, the traffic on Sukhumvit pulled over, and the champion of justice sped off into the night.

———

"What are we looking for?" Daeng was getting tired of driving. "It's three in the morning for heaven's sake."

They'd driven to the night market in Chinatown, the back-packer haven of Khao San Road, a dubious-looking karaoke bar near Nana Plaza, and now they were at the deserted Klong Toey port. At each stop, Daeng would park and wait while they walked around for thirty minutes or so. Each time, Jonathan took his leather briefcase.

The rusty freighters loomed above them as they drove along the pier. A scattering of lights and activity among them attested to the 24-hour maintenance they required. On the deck of one, sparks flew from a welder's torch. The rows of godowns were garishly lit by sodium vapor lights. At the far end of the pier, a lone forklift moved toward a ship's gangplank.

Slowly they cruised. Jonathan had his window down, sniffing the night air like a dog.

Martin eyed him from the back seat. "This is one of his killing fields: 'A lonely sailor is seldom missed.' It's usually assumed he's jumped ship."

Jonathan looked into the shadows. With his vampire eyes, he could see all within. Like looking through an infrared lens, he saw rats scurrying, but nothing else living…or undead.

Daeng had heard this type of talk all night, but neither of them had bothered to explain it to her. "That's it." She slammed on the brakes. "No more driving until you tell me what you are doing."

The car came to a halt at the mouth of an alley leading into the dry dock repair bay. The dry dock was huge, empty, and dark.

"Daeng," Martin spoke. "This isn't the time. I'll explain

everything when we get back." *I'll think of something to tell her.
Lord knows she'll never believe the truth.*

"No. Tell me now." She crossed her arms.

"Daeng. Please—"

"Sshhh." Jonathan was quickly outside the car. "He's here.
Come on. Bring the case." He moved swiftly toward the dry
dock.

"Wait." Martin grabbed the case and started after him. He
turned back to Daeng. "Stay here. And lock the doors." Daeng
stuck her tongue out at him.

And locked the doors.

———

After his rendezvous with Boonsong, Ramonne had finished a
bottle of Beaujolais in the Living Room bar of the Sheraton
Grande, devouring the English-language papers. There was
nothing about him, he was pleased to discover. One article
caught his eye, and he tore it out and placed it in his shirt
pocket, with a smile.

Revenge.

He sauntered along Sukhumvit, stopping for a few glasses
of wine in the so-called "artists bars" on Soi 33 —Café Manet,
Monet, Degas. As he continued on, and the hour grew late, the
crowds thinned out. He could walk for miles without the
slightest exertion, and was so preoccupied with thoughts of
Boonsong and revenge, that he was surprised to see the gray
Eastern Bus Terminal and to realize how far he'd wandered.
Instinctively he headed south to the port. It was time to hunt,
and a drunken sailor or stray hooker would be just the thing to
take his mind off the stinking policeman.

As he entered the port, a long rice barge moved by on the
black river. In the distance, a line of cars crossed the graceful
span of the Rama IX Bridge. The dock appeared deserted, and

Ramonne moved within the shadows. Up ahead, a forklift was making its way to a load of copper cable.

A *tuk-tuk* rolled onto the dock, its annoying little motorcycle engine revving like a machine-gun. Ramonne stayed back in the shadows as two men climbed unsteadily out of the rear. The larger of the two, a red-faced man with a crew cut and a beer belly banged his head on the roof and cursed loudly. His friend, hawk-like and dark, laughed at his misfortune. He paid the driver, who did a 180 and drove off. The crew cut had a beer in his hand, and he held the bottle to the bruise on his forehead. They lurched forward, walking a crooked line toward a gangplank fifty yards ahead.

Ramonne approached them from the rear. "Pardon me. Would you have a light?"

They both stopped and spun around. Ramonne stood, cigarette in hand. *Props.*

The big one with the crew cut fumbled in his pocket and came up with a lighter. Ramonne leaned in, and then turned his face to the man and bared his fangs. Without hearing a word of protest, he had his teeth sunk deep into the man's throat. The beer bottle smashed to the pavement.

"Hey! What the f—" The other drunk made a move to Ramonne.

Without releasing his bite, Ramonne shot out his left arm and gripped the hawk-like man by the neck, choking him in a grip so tight it crushed his larynx.

The man went limp and Ramonne held him by the neck while he continued to drain the big man. With his mouth locked on one man's throat, and the other in his grip, he backed away, dragging them like a wolf would its kill. He headed for the darkness of the dry dock, where he could consume his prey in peace.

———

"He's made a kill," Jonathan said softly.

"How do you know?"

They crouched at the entry to the dry dock. Inside, a half dozen cranes stood silently erect, awaiting their marching orders.

"I feel it. I smell it. He's here. Very close." He opened the case and took out the guns.

Ramonne set down the big man. He would have liked to take his friend's blood, but he, unfortunately, was dead. He would feast only on the blood of the living.

'...here. Very close.'

Ramonne stood up. What was that? Someone was there. *Someone like me. Another forsaken one.*

This was astonishing. In 140 years, he'd seen exactly one other vampire—the one who sired him.

Ramonne leapt straight up to a catwalk twenty feet above his head, and moved silently along it.

Jonathan's eyes showed him the whole of the dry dock. He scanned it, looking into every corner. Cautiously he moved down the cantered floor. He held the dart gun in front of him. Martin followed about ten feet behind.

When Jonathan reached the bottom of the ramp, he sidled in behind the caterpillar tread of a crane. Martin slid in next to him, breathing heavily.

"So close. The kill is..." Jonathan moved around to the front of the crane. "There."

About twenty feet away, two bodies lay slumped at the base of another crane. But Jonathan had no time to dwell on this, as a figure dropped directly onto him.

Jonathan fell to his back and then, with a mighty kick, he threw the assailant off. They both sprang to their feet.

"*You!*" Ramonne hissed.

"Yes, me," Jonathan spat back, raising the dart gun and taking aim.

Ramonne moved faster than the eye could see, and snatched

the weapon away. Stepping back, he studied it… "You'll have to do better than this, boys."

Martin aimed and fired, but the dart whizzed past the vampire's cheek, smashing into the crane. Ramonne whirled and fired directly into Martin's leg. Martin collapsed.

Jonathan leapt, and Ramonne fired point blank at his chest…

As he felt his strength ebb away, Jonathan clutched the vampire by the throat, but soon, he too fell to the floor.

"Boys, boys, boys. Didn't anybody ever tell you it's a man's world." Ramonne tossed away the empty gun.

Martin was unconscious. Out cold. Jonathan was awake, but unable to move. He watched, detached, as Ramonne bent close to him.

The vampire sniffed, long and loud. "I do declare. You've *turned*. Now how is that possible, unless…" He grabbed Jonathan's wrist and turned it over. There was the scar. He sniffed it, too…

"Damn. All I wanted to do was kill you." He looked at Martin's apparently lifeless form. "He's the one I wanted to turn." He walked over and felt the pulse.

Jonathan, though immobile, hissed at Ramonne in warning.

"Easy now. I won't harm him." He stood up, smelled the air… "You're not alone."

———

With long, swift strides, he swept up the ramp and out of the dock.

"Come on. Where are you?" Daeng muttered to herself. "Let's go home. This isn't fun anymore." *What could they possibly be doing in there?*

She turned to look at the alley for the umpteenth time, and she saw him. A tall, Western man, moving straight for the car.

She made sure the doors were locked. They were. She

looked back, and now she could see Jonathan, staggering like he was drunk, trying to catch up with the man.

Before it seemed possible, the man was at the car. He smiled and motioned Daeng to open the door.

She crossed her arms and shook her head.

He smashed his fist through the glass.

Daeng screamed as he wrenched her from the seat and threw her to the pavement. Her head hit the ground hard—and it was probably merciful that she was knocked unconscious.

Ramonne turned to Jonathan who was now at the rear of the car. "Allow me to teach you how to *feed*, boy. It's the least I can do." He picked Daeng up and laid her on the hood of the car.

Jonathan slammed his fist so hard on the trunk that it sprang open.

Ramonne grinned as he raised Daeng's skirt. "Oh, I forgot. You saw me feed on your wife, didn't you?"

Jonathan pulled the shotgun from the golf bag. He pumped a round into the chamber, muttering, "To hell with hallowed ground." He fired just as Ramonne was about to bite into Daeng.

Ramonne turned his head, but the charge ripped off his ear and a good chunk of his left forehead. He hissed, and flew at Jonathan. The blow knocked him off his feet, but Jonathan held onto the shotgun. He pumped it again and fired square into the vampire's chest. The blast lifted Ramonne off him, tossing him twenty feet.

Ramonne looked amazed at the carnage that once was his chest. Chunks of flesh, blood, bone...Armani suit and Donna Karan shirt...all missing. As he struggled to get up, he was shocked that he could look through the holes in his torso and see the car behind.

Jonathan racked the gun again, but Ramonne, missing an ear, a part of his forehead, and with a phone-book-size hole ripped in his chest, leapt thirty feet to the roof of a warehouse and vanished.

Jonathan got up and walked around the car to Daeng. He used the shotgun as a crutch. He was still feeling the tranquilizer dart. Daeng was just coming around.

"You okay?"

"Yes. I guess so. What happened?" She rubbed her head and looked at the broken window on her car.

"Kind of hard to explain. Ask Martin."

"Where *is* Martin?" She looked around.

Martin. Jonathan made a move towards the dry dock when something caught his eye. He bent down and picked it up. It was a newspaper clipping, with a photo. It had been ripped by the shotgun blast to the vampire's chest, and it was singed on one side. He folded it and put it in his pocket.

Then he went after Martin.

23

Fuck me. I look like shit. Ramonne contemplated his image in the gilded Versailles-era mirror. Though it was less than three hours since the encounter, there was already new bone and cartilage forming. The ear was still missing—he thought of the miniature Van Gogh—but the inner ear was re-forming and the missing skull was ringed with a soft shell, like the meat of a coconut. *Amazing.* In 150 years of prowling, stalking, and killing, he'd never once been badly hurt. He'd been scratched, of course, stabbed a couple times, and he'd watched with amazement as the wounds closed, healed, and disappeared overnight. Then there was that time in Pattaya that Jonathan —Jonathan the vampire; he was still in shock at that— had pumped a pistol into him. But those were tiny little holes. The bullets passed right through, and he'd hardly felt the impact.

He had no idea how well-tuned his recuperative properties were. *It's not like they gave me a manual or anything. The Idiot's Guide to Vampiring. How the fuck am I supposed to know? That 400-year-old Chinese cunt told me to get a coffin, hide it, sleep in it, and feed every week at least. As far as making someone a vampire—he fed on me twice—without killing me. That's it. The rest...I've been winging it. For 150 fucking years, thank you very much.*

He had his shirt off. He looked down at his chest. The wounds were healing. Parchment-like scar tissue was stretching across the gaps.

He *had* felt the shotgun blows. They had disoriented him and thrown him off balance. That was new. He'd never felt uncontrolled before. Except of course for those annoying little tranquilizer darts they'd hit him with. *Wonder how they liked a taste of their own fucking medicine?* The forsaken one had, predictably, recovered remarkably fast. He was strong. In that arrogant, newborn way that Ramonne had been strong, also.

The mortal, Martin—*What to do with that boy?*—was no doubt in terrible pain. *Tsk tsk. Shouldn't play with me, boy.*

Vampire hunters? Is that who they thought they were? If this was the worst they could imagine—he took another look in the mirror— he had little to worry about with them. Just let them, and they'd shoot each other.

Satisfied that he would make a full and rapid recovery, Ramonne selected an LP record and put it on the turntable. *Kind of Blue* filled the room. He turned out the lights and climbed into his coffin. As was his custom, he lay in the dark, with the lid open, and cleared his mind.

Revenge. The thought was, oh so sweet.

But to pull it off meant a great sacrifice.

A sacrifice he decided he was ready to make.

———

"Lucy. You got some 'splaining to do."

Every time America's beloved dizzy redhead got in trouble, Ricky would challenge her with that memorable line. Well, this time it was Martin who had some 'splaining to do. And Daeng wasn't letting him off the hook.

Martin had taken her for X-rays right after they left the dockyard. She had a mild concussion, and they had given her pain relievers. He had generally treated her like a princess since the night before. Now he was fluffing her pillows and filling her tumbler of iced water.

"Daeng, you're sure you're okay?"

"Martin. What was that all about?"

Martin sighed, bit the bullet, and told the tale.

He was surprised how the story was now taking on a life of its own. After the second or third time of telling how he'd met and fallen under the spell of a real live vampire, it was becoming more theatrical. Much like, he imagined, screenplays do when they're polished after a third or fourth draft.

Daeng rolled her eyes and said "really?" at all the places that he imagined she would.

When he was finished, she just shook her head. "Martin, Martin, Martin."

He winced. When she said his name *three* times, he knew it was serious.

"If you want to go out and fuck hookers, it's okay with me. Just wear a rubber. That's all I ask. You don't have to make up ridiculous stories. Just go ahead. I really don't care."

And that was the end of it.

————

Jonathan awoke with a splitting headache. He checked the clock —it was after dark—and opened the curtains. Breathing in the night air had no effect. He was almost unable to stand straight; he had such severe cramps.

My God. I have to feed.

He dressed and rode the elevator to the lobby. Outside he turned left on the little *soi* in front of his hotel. To the right was Silom, Patpong, people, action. To the left was quiet, a little neighborhood, old wooden homes and tiny gardens, people gathered around the tube.

And the family dog.

Two dogs seemed to do it. Jonathan was disgusted with himself, but considering the alternative, somewhat proud, also.

He brushed his teeth, flossed, gargled, and went to see Martin.

"Forget the darts. We rip him to shreds with the shotguns, drag the pieces to hallowed ground, and wait for the sun. If any of the pieces move, we blast 'em again." He espoused his new theory to Martin while swigging a glass of *Chateauneuf-du-Pape*. Martin had a case from a recent trip to Provence, and figured it was a lot cheaper to let Jonathan polish it off in his kitchen, than to indulge his new 100-dollar-a-bottle restaurant habit.

"You think that'll work?"

"I think so, yes. He was affected by it. I blew a hole right through him."

"Maybe you killed him?" Martin prayed. "Maybe he crawled off and died."

"Martin, he's a vampire. *I'm* a fucking vampire. I *know* I didn't kill him. Hurt him, yes, but not enough…" He polished off the glass and refilled it. "He'll be back. He's probably grown a new ear already."

"You're looking…" Martin searched for the word. "Well."

Not exactly the right word.

"I fed… Relax. Two stray dogs… At least I think they were strays."

"Yuk."

"I'm strong. We can carry on. That's what matters." He finished the bottle. "How's Daeng?"

"She's fine. A little bruised."

"Did you tell her?"

"Yes. I told her."

"How'd she take it?"

"She chose not to believe it. Typical."

Jonathan arched an eyebrow.

"It's better that way," Martin replied.

"And how are you?"

"I couldn't move for eight hours. I still have a little throbbing, right here." He put a finger to a point on his temple."

Jonathan put his finger where Martin indicated. "Yes. Still some blood coagulated there." He pressed hard and held firm. Martin winced, but when Jonathan released the pressure, it seemed a floodgate was opened in him and Martin felt instant relief.

"That's amazing. Another vampire power?"

Jonathan shook his head. "Acupressure. Tantric studies. I lived in LA once." He smiled.

He opened another bottle and poured a glass for Martin. "Here. I recommend it. And the niacin will do you good."

Martin sipped. "I forgot how good this was."

"Especially after it breathes a while. Opens up your nose to a world of fruits and vines in a lovely French valley. Like sunshine in a bottle." He sighed at the mention of the word sunshine.

Martin changed the subject. "You said you had something important."

Jonathan took out an envelope. Inside was the news clipping he'd found. He handed it to Martin:

AREEYA 'YAYA' BOONSONG SET TO CUT RIBBON AT OPENING OF FIANCÉ'S NEWEST PLEASURE DOME.

A picture of a beautiful young woman with fashionably short hair accompanied the article. It continued with the news that Supachai 'Pee' Lokmon's latest disco, Sound & Light, was officially opening this Friday night, and that the twenty-year-old daughter of Bangrak police's distinguished Lieutenant-Colonel Boonsong, would be cutting the ribbon. It went on to list the young Boonsong's brushes with the law in the past year, all at clubs where illegal drugs were being sold and used. It was all brushed off by her fifty-year-old fiancé as cases of being in the wrong place at the wrong time. Pee expressed relief that Miss Boonsong was now of legal age to attend his club:

"I encourage everyone to come out early and stay until we close."

"Where'd you get this?"

"Ramonne had it. I found it near the car with some ripped bits of his suit." Jonathan put his finger on the picture of the girl. "He's after her. When's Friday?"

Martin looked at his watch. "Tomorrow."

"Daddy's girl." She hated the term. And all it implied. Such as the police escort that followed her most places she went. Under the pretense of protecting her, they no doubt reported back to Daddy on her every move. She deliberately tried to lose them, every chance she got. Signaling for a left and then making a sudden right turn across two lanes of opposing traffic. Or shooting into department-store parking lots without stopping for the ticket, racing into a loading zone, and killing her lights. Then backing down the ramp when the befuddled motorcycle cop passed her by. These exploits often bought her a few precious hours of freedom. Freedom to spend doing drugs with one of her many 'real' boyfriends. More often than not, it merely put another dent in her already worse-for-wear, dark-blue BMW.

Tonight they were behind her, as always, as Yaya pulled into New Petchaburi Road. Why Pee couldn't pick her up, she had no idea. Opening a new club, was for him, about as novel as farting. He had clubs all over the city, four of them in the Royal City Avenue, or RCA, where tonight's festivities would take place. Probably busy bonking one of his new waitresses. Did he think she didn't know? No, she decided, he just didn't care. She was the trophy for years of police pay-offs. She remembered when Daddy introduced them. "Be nice to him," he'd said. Nice. What the fuck did that mean? He'd just gotten her out of a nasty scene with a politician's son and some gunplay in a club. It was just boys showing off, but because of who was involved, the press wanted to make a big deal of it. He had grounded her, but then he told her to get dressed up to meet someone special.

So she'd been nice—and within no time Pee had asked Daddy for her hand in marriage. Never thought to ask her first. Before she knew it, she was wearing a moon-sized diamond and they were an item.

Speaking of rocks, she up-ended a silver inhaler and tooted. The coke gave her an instant rush, and she playfully hit the brakes, causing her motorcycle escort to swerve. She laughed and gave him the finger.

She checked her watch: 10:30. Not bad. Pee told her to be there by 10:00. She'd be there by 11:00. In Thai time they were both the same. She knew that if she had shown up at 10:00, Pee would be nowhere in sight, and everyone would wonder why she was there so early?

Eminem came on the stereo and she turned it up. She sang along and danced in her seat.

———

Jonathan checked the time: 10:15. "Where is she?"

"I told you." Martin smiled.

The newspaper had promised a grand ribbon-cutting ceremony at ten o'clock sharp. Jonathan had gone out with the setting sun and scored another couple of neighborhood dogs, and been round to pick up Martin by nine o'clock. By 9:45, they pulled into a dusty lot across from the twin klieg lights outside Sound & Light. Martin avoided the valet parking and chose a spot that he could get out of easily. They strode up to join the throng of press and gawkers. Under their jackets, they each had a 12-gauge, sawed-off shotgun with full magazine. Riot guns.

For a grand opening, the club looked remarkably 'open' already. VIPs flashed invitations and strode through a security checkpoint of shapely young girls in black hotpants and tight S & L T-shirts. Inside, there already appeared to be several hundred assorted big-shots. The press set off their strobe lights like Chinese firecrackers every time a pop star appeared, and politely nodded or *waied* to a member of parliament. Tata Young sold papers, the deputy minister of communications did not.

Jonathan had almost completely mastered his extra-sensory perceptions, and could shut out the crowd. He studied the faces of the mainly teenage or early twenties crowd. Those entering the club were fashionably dressed, predominately in black, and drove or were driven in expensive cars. Those watching them had the look of hunger. Starved for a glimpse of a celebrity, a taste of the good life, a crumb from the plate of the elite. The girls screamed in unison if one of their idols deemed them worthy of a glance their way.

He felt no trace of Ramonne.

For a club called Sound & Light, the event so far was pretty quiet. That was just the way Pee Lokmon wanted it. Known simply as "The Man" to those who worked for him—The Man doesn't like that color; The Man needs his car—Pee would turn on the 10,000 giga-watt system himself. Right after Yaya cut the ribbon. Until then the guests mingled and drank free champagne while muted music played under soft lights.

Pee ran a hand over his cleanly shaven head. Bruce Willis was right when he called the shaved head the "comb-over of the current day." Pee loved it, though. It reminded him of that basketball player—Kareem somebody…? Never mind. At least now he wasn't going bald anymore. He passed through the crowd, shaking hands and clinking his glass with an endless stream of well-wishers, their consorts, concubines, girlfriends, boyfriends, and assorted hangers-on. Most he knew personally, and their wishes of success were sincere and heartfelt. Others were what he referred to as "this year's crop," and he knew that they probably wouldn't even have the price of admission in a year. He virtually ignored them. He'd been in the club business for twenty years, and had the two things you needed to succeed. A pair of brass balls.

One sullen young man with intense eyes, who ignored the free champagne and bought a bottle of expensive red wine, intrigued him…and he almost introduced himself.

Ramonne was glad that the music was low. It was his worst fear that he'd spend hours in some intolerable disco hell. He loved music, and was appalled at what was being passed off under that umbrella these days. He enjoyed watching the *crème de la crème* of Bangkok's young social set strutting their stuff. He saw lots of sleek white necks and creamy long legs that he would just love to sink his teeth into. But, just to be sure of controlling himself, he had fed early tonight. He observed the owner, a handsome Thai-Chinese in a nicely tailored Hugo Boss suit, doing his job of pressing the flesh. He thought for a moment the man was going to come over and introduce himself.

Ramonne knew that he wouldn't have a chance with her if he approached her outside. But in here, he felt confident it would be different. He was contemplating his plan, when he was aware of a presence.

"Pee Lokmon. Welcome to Sound & Light."

A hand was extended in front of his face. Ramonne studied it for a moment, and then took it and shook it lightly.

"Ramonne Delacroix. Thank you."

"I don't believe we've met before?" Which meant, who are you, asshole, and what are you doing at my private party.

"No. I'm a friend of Areeya's father." Ramonne smiled.

"Ahh. Well, any friend of Lieutenant-Colonel Boonsong is *most* welcome."

"Thank you. Is she here yet?"

"No. But I expect her shortly. Please, come to my private room. I'll bring her there after we officially open."

Pee escorted Ramonne to a large, soundproof room that overlooked the dance floor. It was full of The Man's closest associates— mostly middle-aged men in black business suits— and plenty of beautiful young girls. He ordered another bottle of the Volnay-Santenots that Ramonne was drinking—"My compliments"—and assured Ramonne that Yaya would be up to see him shortly. Then Pee left to get on with the festivities.

What a gracious host. The vampire settled into the comfortable VIP lounge to await his prey. He sipped his wine and surveyed the activity below.

———

Yaya pulled into the front of the club and was met by Lek, Pee's personal bodyguard. He ushered her to a podium in front of two huge doors bearing the Sound & Light logo with a big pink ribbon stretched across them. Pee arrived and kissed her on both cheeks. A pink spotlight was trained on the podium, and Yaya squinted as she stepped into its glare. Pee leaned into a bank of microphones. "Ladies and gentlemen of Bangkok. It is time to parrteee!" His trademark line. He handed an oversize pair of scissors to Yaya, and she hacked through the ribbon. The minute she did, the doors flew open and hundreds of pink balloons floated out and up over the heads of the madly cheering crowd.

Glad that that nonsense was over, Yaya hooked her arm with Pee's and allowed him to escort her into the club proper.

———

"Where is he?" Martin shouted. The noise of the crowd was now deafening, and they were being swept up in a wave that was rushing for the opened door.

"I don't know," Jonathan confessed. "This is all so confusing."

With the crowd pushing and shoving him, Martin kept a tight grip on his riot gun under his jacket. *How will we find him?*

"He's here. I feel him. He must be inside."

They went with the flow and were soon in the club. The place was quickly swelling to capacity. Shoulder to shoulder, wall to wall.

A spotlight focused on a figure in the glass suite above the crowd. A voice boomed over the speakers. It was The Man again. "Ladies and gentlemen. Thank you all for coming tonight. Welcome to Sound & Light. Bangkok's newest, loudest, sexiest nightclub!"

With each word, the crowd on the floor roared its approval.

"Are you ready to parrteee?"

Another roar.

"I can't *hear* you. I said…are you ready to *parrrteeee*?"

This time the roar was deafening.

"That's more like it. Ladies and gentlemen…I give you the Sound & Light dancers."

Four red spotlights hit each corner of the dance floor, as four cages descended. In each cage were two blonde Russian bombshells. Red T-shirts and red hotpants. They bumped and ground to a pulsating rhythm. The roar of approval went up a notch.

Jonathan stood on a staircase, scanning the crowd… Lots of freaks, but no vampire.

"And now, let's fire up the Sound & Light laser system!"

Laser pods descended around the dance floor, and green beams swept the crowd. Then a huge spaceship dropped from the center point and hovered. It slowly spun, and lights of every size, shape, and color slashed through the club. Strobes randomly fired, giving the suggestion of a battlefield.

"And *now*, the loudest, baddest sound system in all of Asia. Ladies and gentlemen…it is definitely time to *paarrrrtteeeee*!"

The floor began to vibrate at a low frequency. It grew

louder and the tremors increased. Soon it moved up from the floor to the walls. Then the pounding, pumping, thumping bass. Those within ten feet of the wall—which housed the bass speakers— felt as if the sound was forcing them toward the dance floor.

Jennifer Lopez sang a single lyric over and over, through the 360-degree speakers, and when the full sound of the music finally kicked in, the effect was overwhelming. People were literally lifted up and compelled to dance. The beat pulsated through everything—every table, every chair, every leg, every limb.

Martin felt the bass pounding in his back, right between the shoulder blades. The rhythm lifted his feet, and Jennifer Lopez...she was right inside his head, singing to him. Martin *never* danced, but he couldn't help himself. He jerked and swayed in time with the overwhelming sound.

The lights flashed and changed with the music; the Russian dolls shimmied and shook their asses off. Everybody was going mad. Especially Jonathan. It was all too much for him. He had his fingers in his ears as he continued to scan the crowd.

———

True to his word, Pee appeared in the VIP lounge with Yaya, and walked her over to Ramonne. He deposited her on the couch, and without a word, headed for the window that overlooked the dance floor. He picked up a microphone and proceeded to "Start the parrtee!"

Yaya ignored Ramonne, looking in her bag.

Ramonne sipped his wine while Pee did his thing.

She produced a pack of cigarettes. Drawing one out, she turned to Ramonne. "Light?"

Ramonne produced a silver lighter. *Props.*

"You shouldn't smoke," he advised as he leaned close to her.

"Yeah...? I shouldn't do lots of things, but I do." She lit the cigarette and blew a stream of smoke through pursed, dark-cherry lips.

"Do I know you?" She looked at him accusingly.

"Ramonne Delacroix. I'm an acquaintance of your father."

"Oh yeah? Cop or crook?" She gave a cynical laugh.

"Neither, I assure you."

Something about him put her at ease. Pee was safely wrapped up, showing off the lights of the club. Daddy's motorcycle escort was having a cigarette break outside. But then an awful thought occurred to her. What if this was her father's inside man tonight? A very handsome, sophisticated, charming, *French* cop…? She laughed at herself, but just the same she had to ask. "Did—?"

"No," Ramonne assured her. "Your father did not hire me to watch you."

"How did you know what I was going to ask?"

"I read it on your face. I read a lot in people's faces."

"For instance…" He studied her. "You are a very precocious young lady. Fiercely independent, resentful of authority, especially your father. You'd like nothing better than to escape his control, but you don't know how. So you've agreed to marry a man that you don't love, just to get away from your father." Ramonne sipped his wine and awaited her response.

It didn't come right away. First she snapped her fingers at a passing waitress and took two flutes of champagne. She offered one to Ramonne. He took it and they clinked glasses.

"*Touché*. You're the first man that has ever understood me, and you did it in less than five minutes." She downed her champagne. Ramonne put his down.

She pointed at the glass.

Ramonne smiled and shrugged. "I don't drink…champagne." He picked up his glass of red and saluted her before downing it in one gulp. "Ahhh. Lovely."

She took the other glass of champagne. "Drinking buddies?" She lightly knocked his glass with hers.

He smiled. "Drinking buddies."

"Good," she replied. "I love to drink." And she finished off the second glass. "Now, tell me about you." She snapped her fingers again at the waitress.

"Not much to tell. Born in France. Went off to see the world. Landed in Thailand. And here I am."

Two more glasses were set in front of her. When Pee had made the final announcement…"And *now*, the loudest, baddest sound system in all of Asia…" the place went off the Richter scale. The vibrations set the glasses dancing across the table.

Yaya wrinkled her nose and jerked a thumb toward Pee, who was basking in the spotlight and throwing kisses while the crowd jerked and spasmed.

"Just look at boy wonder and his new toy. Some men need big cars, some need big cigars. Pee needs big sound systems. Luckily we're insulated against it. Imagine what it's like down there."

Ramonne shook his head. He could imagine it. If he wanted to. "You're young. Don't you like this—" He found he couldn't say the word 'music.'

"I like it, but I know this techno trance shit isn't music. It just moves the masses. Give me enough drugs…the *right* drugs, and I'm right there with them. Boogie 'til you puke. Right now, though, I'm perfectly comfortable right here."

She put her hand over his. There was definitely something about this man. She sat closer. "Unless of course, you *want* to go down there."

"No. No. I too am very happy right here."

She was much more than he expected. She was narcissistic, she relied on artificial stimulants—these things he expected—but he didn't expect she'd be so…charming. Yes. That was the word. He was being charmed by her.

And then The Man was back. "How do you like my club?" He slid in next to Yaya and put a protective arm around her shoulder.

For the first time, Ramonne noticed that Pee had a solid gold tooth, right in the center of his upper palate. There seemed to be a tiny diamond in the center.

Ridiculous.

"Very charming." Ramonne looked directly at Yaya as he said the words.

Pee was obviously pumped up and reveling in his glory. In the thickly padded comfort of the VIP lounge, you could feel but not really hear the techno beat. You could observe the crowd if you chose to, but you had to walk to the floor-to-ceiling windows on the other side of the leather booths. There, like Caesar in the arena, you could gaze down upon the masses and watch the light spill across them. You could see, if you chose to, the Russian dancers tease them, and see the music drive them with its primal beat.

"Membership in the VIP club will be a million baht. For that you get a lifetime card. I hope it's a long one." Pee laughed at his little joke. No one had paid the absurd fee as yet, but it certainly sounded good when bestowing gratis membership on various members of parliament and the media.

Ramonne thought the joke ironic. *What is a lifetime to these mortals? Seventy-five years?* Perhaps he should buy a membership. He would be the only one to get his money's worth. *Eternal life membership.*

He laughed out loud.

"Ahhh, you like my little joke." Pee crossed his arms and smiled.

"Yes." Ramonne looked him in the eye. "You're a funny man. Absurd, actually."

Yaya gave him a curious look. Now what? This man was really unpredictable.

"Oh? And just *what* is so absurd?" Pee uncrossed his arms and leaned forward. A vein popped on his forehead.

Pee, on the other hand, was totally *predictable.*

"The absurd notion that I should give a shit about you because you own a fucking disco."

"*What?*" Pee could not believe what he was hearing.

"I'm just here for the girl, old man. You should be home watching TV with the rest of the geriatrics."

Now there was a glazed look acrosss Pee's face. It was almost as if he could not comprehend what this rude *farang* was saying. As if the sounds were audible but his brain was not responding to the meaning. But there was no mistaking the tone, and he stood up.

Yaya couldn't believe what she'd heard either. He had to be crazy. But he *was* very sexy.

Ramonne started to rise, but she took his hand and restrained him. "No, don't."

Pee motioned and two giant men in black stepped forward. The goons each put a hand on Ramonne's shoulder. Let's be reasonable, they seemed to imply.

Ramonne smiled and stood. And then—faster than anyone could see—he flipped first one, and then the other, through the plate-glass, where they crashed onto the dance floor below.

———

With the crashing glass, Jonathan whirled and saw the vampire standing in a room full of shocked faces. "*There!*" He sprinted to the staircase. Martin, fighting the crowd, was right behind him.

"Come, my dear. We're leaving." Ramonne offered his hand to

Yaya.

Pee was dumbfounded. "Areeya. Please… This is my night."

Yaya had no idea what to do.

So Ramonne helped her. He grabbed her by the hand and led her toward the nearest exit… Just as Jonathan came into the lounge, shotgun at the ready.

"Ramonne!"

The vampire turned, hissed, and then lifted Yaya and put her behind the bar. He leapt for Jonathan, who pulled the trigger.

In mid-air, Ramonne dodged the blast, which destroyed a fine display of premium vodkas. He landed in front of Martin.

Time seemed suspended. Ramonne's eyes locked on Martin. They bored into his head. The room started to spin.

Martin leveled his gun…but couldn't fire.

"You disappoint me, boy." He turned his back and started for

Jonathan.

Now Martin fired, but again Ramonne dodged the charge.

By now, the crowd was panicking and stampeding for the exit. Ramonne swung on an art deco chandelier and knocked Jonathan's weapon to the ground, before landing at the feet of the shocked Yaya.

"Time to go." He grabbed her and turned.

Jonathan retrieved his gun, but held his fire. Ramonne smiled, and then, with the girl over his shoulder, he leapt through a smoked-glass window, thirty feet to the parking lot below.

Jonathan ran to the broken window and could only watch as the vampire carried another victim into the night.

25

"I suppose I should thank you. You tried to save my daughter."

Boonsong directed this to Martin and Jonathan, but his eyes were on Nao, the uniformed cop who'd followed Yaya to the club, but remained outside during her abduction.

Boonsong startled them both with his opening statement.

Martin had been certain that his re-arrest was imminent. He shifted nervously. He'd been pale with anxiety from the moment the police seized him and Jonathan. He feared the worst. The two officers told them nothing on the ride to Bangrak Police Station.

But Jonathan could come in handy, he thought. *A vampire on my side.*

"Why were you there?" Boonsong asked.

"To protect your daughter," Martin quickly answered.

"Oh? And what made you think that she needed protection?"

"I found a clipping about her, in Ramonne's—" He wasn't sure what else to call him. "In his possession. I thought he might mean to harm her."

"Why didn't you inform me of this?"

"Pardon me, but you and I have not had the most cordial

relationship. I'm out on bail at the moment, on charges you filed."

"And I could put you back in a cell right now for any number of violations. Concealed weapons, for starters."

On Boonsong's desk were the two riot guns and their shells.

He glared at Martin. And then motioned to Sergeant Thamarat to clear the room. The sergeant escorted Officer Nao, who was glad to be leaving, and left them alone.

Boonsong opened his desk drawer and produced a parchment envelope. He handed it to Martin. "This arrived tonight. Right after the kidnapping." Martin recognized the calligraphy immediately.

Khun Boonsong,

Your daughter is safe. I will not harm her. I propose an exchange. Your life for hers. Tomorrow night. Wat Arun pier. Midnight. Come alone.

R.

"What do you know of this man?" Boonsong took the note back.

"Well, for one thing…he's a man, yes, but he's not human."

"It's true, then." Boonsong moaned. "He is *phii dib.*"

"If that means vampire, yeah," Jonathan chimed in.

Martin nodded. He knew the Thai word for ghosts who sucked blood. It figured in the folklore.

"I thought he was just a deviate," Boonsong offered. "A maniac who made his crimes appear the work of a ghost." I like to think I'm a modern man. Forensic science, DNA…that's the future of criminology, I believe. A *phii dib*? That I do not believe."

"But why? Why did you let him carry out his crimes? Surely you could have stopped him?"

"If what you're telling me is true, then *how* would I stop him?"

"Point," Martin conceded. "But you could have exposed him."

Boonsong sighed. "Mr. Larue. You are still a defendant in a murder case. Anything I'm saying here is off the record. I will deny it in court." He turned to Jonathan. "And you, Mr. Peyton. You, I will simply eliminate."

Go ahead and try, big boy.

"Having said that, it was…profitable for me to ignore Mr. Delacroix's indiscretions—"

"Indiscretions! He's a serial killer. A very prolific serial killer." Martin was enraged.

"As I said. I chose to ignore what he was doing in exchange for a contribution. His contributions grew larger as time went by."

"As did his indiscretions."

"Yes. I grant you that. But, Mr. Larue, understand my position. Mr. Delacroix preyed upon the dregs of society. The throw-offs. The strays. The drug abusers. Prostitutes. Life's unwanted. Rarely did I receive a request, even, for the body. Much less an autopsy or any examination. In a way, he…performed a service."

Martin glared at Boonsong. "That's despicable."

Boonsong merely shrugged shoulders and eyebrows.

"But now, I take it, he's crossed the line," Jonathan offered.

"He has *my daughter.*" Boonsong's eyes narrowed. "Yes. I want him *now.* I want him stopped."

"So do we."

"My entire force is combing the city, but I doubt they'll find him." He sat down in his chair, his hands on the desk. "So what do we do?"

"You show us yours, we'll show you ours," Martin offered.

———

A guest. Ramonne had a guest. His first ever.

He tried to be hospitable, but she kept screaming and trying to escape. So he had to tie and gag her. Now she looked remarkably uncomfortable.

"*Tsk tsk tsk*. I really was hoping that we could continue our conversation."

Yaya nodded.

"You promise not to scream." He read her thoughts.

She nodded again, and he removed the silk scarf from her lovely mouth.

"Who *are* you?" She glared at him. Her hands were still tied with silk cords to the arms of a gold-leafed Louis XIV armchair. Her ankles were bound likewise.

"I told you, Ramonne Delacroix."

"Okay. *What* are you?"

Ramonne sat in a chair opposite her. "I go by many names. The Dark Angel. The Forsaken One. The Undead. But most commonly, a vampire."

Yaya tensed in her chair. She fought with the cords binding her. Her heart raced.

"Relax, my dear. I mean *you* no harm."

"Why have you brought me here?"

"You're but a pawn in a game. It's your father that I want."

"What do you have to do with my father?"

"Your father and I have played a game for a long time. It's time for the game to end."

"I don't understand."

"I don't expect you to, my dear. It is enough for you to know that you will not be harmed, and that tomorrow night you will be exchanged for your father."

"Then what?"

"What do you mean?"

"What will you do with my father?"

"Again, that doesn't concern you. I have a score to settle with him."

"You're going to kill him, aren't you?"

Ramonne didn't answer immediately. He looked at her eyes. There were tears there.

"No."

"Yes you are. You're a monster." She began screaming again

Ramonne sighed and replaced the silken gag. "I really felt we had something going back there at the club. Pity you insist on all the hysterics. Not that anyone can hear you. But just the same, I'll not get a minute's rest if you keep up that racket."

While Yaya watched wide-eyed, Ramonne opened the lid to his coffin and climbed in. She emitted a muffled scream as he closed the lid and the lights went out.

———

It was almost dawn when they had finished their shared tales of Ramonne. Jonathan told of his encounter in Pattaya, but omitted his recent conversion to the dark side. He successfully managed to return to his hotel before daylight by claiming to be a diabetic in dire need of his medicine.

By this point, Martin had devised a plan. A plan that would require the co-operation of a number of Boonsong's men. A plan that assured he'd get little rest before tonight's midnight rendezvous.

A plan that he hoped and prayed would work.

26

A full moon on the Chao Phraya sent golden waves undulating behind a ponderous rice barge. Promptly at midnight the flood-lights were extinguished at Wat Arun, the Temple of Dawn, and only the silver orb illuminated the man standing alone on the pier.

Lieutenant-Colonel Boonsong was unarmed. Well…he had a small .22-caliber pistol clipped inside his boot, but that hardly counted. Besides, knowing what he now knew, what possible good would it do?

He would face this demon alone, as he requested. He would not put his daughter's life in jeopardy. This he vowed.

As the barge passed, Boonsong heard the steady drone of a powerboat approaching. He couldn't see the smaller craft until the barge was gone. Then, a *reua hang yao*, or *klong* boat, could be seen approaching the pier. It appeared to have two occupants plus the helmsman. As it got closer, he recognized the vampire standing near the long sloping bow, with Boonsong's daughter seated in front of him.

His blood began to boil. If the vampire had harmed her…

But he knew he was impotent. He must wait. Play the game by the vampire's rules.

The boatman cut the engine and the longtail rocked up to the pier.

"*Por!*" Yaya cried out.

"Are you all right?" he called in turn.

"Your daughter is fine. I told you that I would not harm her." Ramonne stepped off the boat and held a hand out to help her up.

"Daddy. He's going to kill you!" she shrieked as she stepped on the pier and rushed to his arms.

Boonsong hugged her as the tears flowed. Finally he held her at arm's length and looked her over. "You're all right?"

"Yes. Just scared."

"Don't worry. Everything will be fine."

"Yes, Areeya. Everything will be fine. Your father and I have some unfinished business to attend to. Don't we, Colonel...?" Ramonne motioned to the boat.

"Don't Daddy. Don't go with him!" Yaya grabbed her father's arm and held on tightly.

Gently, Boonsong took her hand and removed it. "It's all right. Don't be afraid."

Ramonne smiled with delight as the lieutenant-colonel started for the boat.

Suddenly an explosion shattered the silence of the night.

All eyes turned to the sound, as Jonathan stepped out from the shadow of the temple, smoking shotgun in his hand. As he racked another round into the chamber, Martin emerged, bearing his own riot gun.

"Well, well, well. It's the vampire hunters. Surprise, surprise." Ramonne smiled and crossed his arms.

"Colonel, help your daughter into the boat," Jonathan commanded. He kept the shotgun pointed at Ramonne.

Yaya turned to her father. "Daddy? Who are these men?"

"Get in." He held her hand and she climbed back into the boat. The skipper cowered in the stern.

Ramonne was completely calm as he stared down the barrels of two shotguns.

Martin waved his gun at the boatman, who threw his hands into the air and started to chant.

"*Pai* Tha Tien," Martin instructed, telling him to take Yaya to the pier on the opposite bank.

The man started the engine and roared away from the dock, glad to make his escape. The hapless Yaya could only stare at them as the boat took her away.

"That was my ride." Ramonne scowled.

"You won't be needing it."

"Oh? And why is that?"

"Because you won't be leaving here," Jonathan replied.

"And what will keep me here?"

As he said the words, he smelled the first wisps of smoke. He turned to see the saffron-robed monks with torches who were now setting fire to huge piles of cut logs.

"*That* will keep you here."

Ramonne knew what this meant, and he watched in amazement as the rear of the temple grounds was ringed in twenty-foot-high flames. This effectively made an island of the temple —fire on one side, the river on the other.

Jonathan didn't see the vampire move. Ramonne pounced on him, smashing the gun from his hand. He held the young vampire to the ground, his hands tight around his throat. "How are you feeling, *boy*?" He looked into his eyes and read the pain behind them. "You don't like being one of us, do you?"

Boonsong reached into his boot, pulled out the .22 pistol, but seemed hesitant to fire. He looked back and forth between the boat now approaching the other side and the two men on the ground. Martin, also reluctant to fire, swung his gun by the barrel, trying to club Ramonne with it.

He was rewarded for his effort as Ramonne swatted him like a fly. He landed twenty feet away near the water.

Ramonne sniffed and snorted. "*Dogs*…? You feed on dogs?"

Jonathan gave a loud howl and flung the vampire off. Ramonne landed on his back, with a look of surprise. "You're strong, boy."

Jonathan snatched back his gun and fired. Ramonne dodged the shot, and before Jonathan could re-load, he came at him. Jonathan swung the gun like a baseball bat, smashing Ramonne hard in the face and knocking him to the ground.

Ramonne shook his head, growled, and then leapt forty feet up the steps of the giant *chedi*. Jonathan followed him up the great temple, but Ramonne kicked sideways and knocked him off balance. He pinned him down with a boot heel on his chest. "More than you bargained for, isn't it?" He laughed…mocking him.

Jonathan brought his foot up hard into Ramonne's groin, enough to free himself and get to his feet.

In three quick bounds, Ramonne reached the pinnacle of the temple, where he sat watching as Jonathan crouched and prepared to leap at him.

"Dogs? Didn't you learn anything from me? Your wife… now she was a meal."

Jonathan snarled with rage and pounced.

Ramonne braced himself and met the young vampire with a powerful thrust of both legs. The blow caught Jonathan in mid-air and sent him hurtling 200 feet to the pavement below. He landed on his back with a sickening *crack*!

Ramonne smiled as Jonathan lay there, unable to move.

Martin, still recovering himself, went to his friend. Jonathan's eyes were open, and he grimaced in pain.

The smoke from the fires blew across him as Ramonne started to descend. "*Youth*. 'Tis a pity it's wasted on the young. The boy is strong. But not strong enough."

Martin picked up his shotgun and stood.

"Not yet, *boy*." Ramonne was at the mid-way point.

Martin aimed, but was certain he was out of range. Boonsong held the small revolver on the vampire.

"No, not yet."

Ramonne started to walk down the remaining steps, and then leapt straight for Boonsong.

Boonsong fired his pistol, the gun having no effect.

The vampire ripped open the lieutenant-colonel's throat and began to devour him. Unable to get a clear shot, Martin moved in close.

Ramonne released his bite on Boonsong, but for only a fleeting moment, turning his blazing yellow eyes onto Martin. He reached out at astonishing speed, and snatched the barrel of the shotgun. He pointed it to the sky, then resumed his death-grip on Boonsong's throat.

Martin held onto the gun, struggling to turn it on Ramonne, but the vampire's grip was like steel. Finally, the lieutenant-colonel was dead, and Ramonne withdrew his fangs. He let the body slide from his grasp, while still gripping the shotgun. Rivulets of blood ran down from the corners of his mouth onto his silk shirt. He turned to face Martin. "Now," he said. And released the grip on the gun.

Trembling with fear, tears of grief watering his eyes, Martin raised the gun. But his finger on the trigger was now immobile. It wouldn't move.

"I can't." He started to put the gun down.

Ramonne's eyes narrowed as he focused on Martin. "Be strong, boy."

Martin's finger jerked like it was hit by lightning. The gun fired at point blank range, the vampire's head exploded in a sphere of blood.

The headless corpse crashed to the ground and Martin sank to his knees.

———

The first rosy fingers of light moved through the now smoldering fires, and across the grounds of the Temple of

Dawn. Martin sat at the temple's base, his back to the rising sun. He had kept a silent vigil through the early morning hours.

Towards sunrise, Jonathan had spoken quietly to him. Martin honored the pact they had entered into in the hours before midnight.

He watched in wonder as the rays of the sun slowly incinerated the two decapitated corpses lying before him. In only a matter of minutes, they were turned to ashes. A gentle breeze blew them across the hallowed ground, over the bare feet of the monks who arrived for morning prayers, and into the river.

EPILOGUE

The thirteenth-century Temple of Bayon stood frozen in time, wrapped with huge, swollen vines as the jungle embraced and claimed the stone. The roots of a giant banyan tree up-ended blocks of sandstone weighing two or more tons. Apsaras danced around the lintels, and the Mona Lisa face of King Jayavarman adorned its pagodas...

The silver and tin image was encased in a simple teak frame. It had long been said that Henri Mouhot had actually photographed the temples of Angkor—Mouhot had practiced under the tutelage of Louis Daguerre himself—but until this moment, the rumor of the daguerreotype images' existence had never been proven.

Martin now gazed at a dozen of them.

None had ever been seen before, because Ramonne Delacroix had taken the negative plates with him when he left Cambodia in

1860.

Martin turned on another Tiffany lamp and moved from photo to photo in awe. He looked again at the letter:

Dear Martin,

If you are reading this, then my assumptions were correct. You, of course, knew that Wat Arun stands upon what is constituted as hallowed ground, and that the means of my destruction were at hand. What you did not know was that I was your willing accomplice.

One hundred and seventy seven years is quite long enough, Martin. I have grown weary of this life. Weary of this world. I've seen man descend from being an active participant who lusted after the new and the unexplored, to the generations now who sit in phosphorescent rooms, their eyes glued to one of a variety of glowing tubes.

The cities that man once took pride in constructing—Paris and London in the nineteenth century, Krung Thep when I first arrived— are now uninhabitable sewers that pollute the very soul.

I have also grown weary, alas, of the hunt. Perhaps it was you, but something made me assess the force I am predisposed to satiate in order to maintain my very existence. I have begun to take pity on my victims. A very taxing demeanor for a forsaken one.

And so, dear friend, once trusted comrade, I leave my departure in your capable hands.

Herein are a map, a key, and several bank account numbers. Notes have been sent to the managers to release all funds at your instruction. Follow the map to my humble abode. The contents within represent the attempt to recapture the living soul I gave up that terrible night, so long ago, in a faraway jungle.

R.

The note had been waiting at Martin's apartment when he finally returned. Boonsong had also left a note—admitting all; naming names, dates, and places; and exonerating Martin of all guilt or complicity.

Had the lieutenant-colonel survived the night, Martin wondered whether the note would have surfaced at all?

But the point was moot now.

Martin went to Lumpini Stadium. A groundskeeper let him in, for a small fee, of course, and he found his way in the underground passage to an unmarked door.

The key turned the lock, and he entered Ramonne's lair.

What lay within was probably akin, Martin surmised, to one of the storage chambers in the basement of the Louvre: a Van Gogh; two Renoir ballerina pastels; the daguerreotypes, including others of Paris and African wildlife; hundreds of bottles of vintage red wines; Tiffany lamps; Fabergé eggs; carved jade, intricate ivory sculpture; a pristine stereo with a Bang & Olufsen turntable, an AR tuner, and Bose speakers; hundreds of LPs, all jazz and classical; hundreds of books, most of them rare, cloth-bound first editions.

Why did Ramonne need my money?

As soon as Martin raised the question, he knew the answer. He didn't. He needed the companionship. The willing ear. The need to share his memories. He was more human than one would ever have thought.

The coffin, the centerpiece of the room, was unorthodox to say the least. Martin lifted the lid and peered into the satin interior. Lying on the pillow was a small remote control. Martin picked it up, realizing it was for the stereo, and instinctively pushed play.

Across the room, the tone arm set gently into the groove, and a very soft, warm sound came from the speakers... Chet Baker's hushed horn floated into the room.

Martin sat in the Louis XIV armchair, noting the soft silken cords still looped around the arms, and listened...

This, Martin, this is music... This man knew how to move you to tears with the simple elegance of a brass horn. You know the instrument... Three valves are all it has to control the sound. All is accomplished through lip and breath control. The player must become the music.

Martin remembered listening to the same track in Brown Sugar, with Ramonne, on that first night together, *so long ago.*

Under Ramonne's spell, Martin had thought the music magical. But then Ramonne had started ranting about the inferior quality of digitized music. "Blasphemous" had been his exact word.

He was right, of course. There was the occasional pop or hiss, but the sound coming through the speakers now was richer and fuller than anything he'd heard in years.

He drifted with the music, examining books, paintings, and jewelry until he was exhausted. He realized he hadn't slept in 48 hours.

He thought of climbing in the coffin, just try it for size, but more sensible thoughts prevailed, once again.

He turned out the lights, locked the door, and bid goodbye to a friend.

AUTHOR'S NOTE

The tale just told is a work of fiction. Vampires do not exist in Bangkok or any other city ...as far as we know.

ABOUT THE AUTHOR

Jim Newport is a writer and Emmy-nominated production designer of both film and television. His film credits include *Bangkok Dangerous*, *Brokedown Palace*, *The Stepfather* and *Heart Like A Wheel*. In television he has set the "look" for many series by designing the pilot episodes of *The Lyon's Den, The Shield, The Education Of Max Bickford* and *China Beach*. His work on *The Piano Lesson* for the Hallmark Hall Of Fame was nominated for an Emmy in art direction. He was the production designer of season four of the worldwide hit TV series *Lost*. When not writing books or designing films, Newport performs as his alter-ego Jimmy Fame—a blues shouter, known to haunt the saloons and annual Blues Festival of his adopted home, Phuket, Thailand.

Please visit the author's website: www.vampireofsiam.com.

THE VAMPIRE OF SIAM SERIES

The Vampire of Siam series is an epic tale that spans half the globe and a course of 150 years.

In *The Vampire of Siam* (Book 1) a nineteenth-century explorer, Ramonne Delacroix, encounters an ancient Chinese demon in the temples of Angkor Wat. His subsequent nocturnal transformation leads him to the capital of Siam, where he witnesses the coronation of kings and the city's metamorphosis into the modern day sin-city of Bangkok.

Living the life of the lone hunter for the first 145 years of his incarnation as a night stalker, the vampire is reborn in *Ramonne* (Book 2) and eventually seeks to know the true extent of his powers. As he learns, he evolves. By the second book's end, the vampire's strength is enormous and he has control of the true magic he has been vested with.

In *The Reckoning* (Book 3) Ramonne, armed with newfound knowledge, seeks the source of his powers. He journeys back to Cambodia and the ancient temples to a fateful encounter with Zhoupeng—the mighty devil who "turned him" so many years before. Ramonne vows to put an end to Zhoupeng's reign of evil over the poor land.

Throughout the three books, Ramonne's fate is inextricably entwined with that of Martin Larue—wealthy American expat. Drawn to each other by mutual admiration and fascination, they eventually end up relying on each other to sort out the twisted path they find themselves thrust upon.

Together they face vampire-hunters, corrupt cops, opium dens, bordellos, blind fortune-tellers, jealous lovers, terrorists, suicide-bombers, smugglers, warlords and soul-sucking demons.

The Siamese Connection (Book 4) begins in 1948 Bangkok, shortly after the end of WWII and the Japanese occupation of Siam. The vampire, Ramonne Delacroix becomes involved in a quest for a mysterious artifact—The Oracle—hidden during the war by the Japanese. He joins forces with the famous American Expat Jim Thompson, (before he was the Silk King he was an OSS agent) and together they do battle with the nefarious Japanese Black Dragons.

The tale continues in the present day picking up where *The Reckoning* left off. Martin Larue and his pregnant wife Areeya cross paths again with the vampire and soon they too are involved in a deadly game of cat and mouse with the descendants of the Black Dragons, who are still in search of the mysterious Oracle.

A fast-paced blend of fact and fiction, *The Siamese Connection* finally solves the mysterious disappearance of Jim Thompson.

"Newport artfully shapes the vampire legend into a Mekong cocktail of surprises." Christopher G. Moore.

CHASING JIMI

Chasing Jimi is a rock 'n' roll period piece. It spans one year - the summer of 1966 to the summer of 1967. From New York's Greenwich Village to swinging London to the stage of the Monterey Pop Festival. It follows the ascension of one Jimmy James, a struggling back-up guitar player, to the exalted throne of rock-god superstardom.

On the road through merry-old England with the re-named Jimi Hendrix we meet the madcap royalty of the British pop scene. Jimi forms an endearing friendship with Rolling Stones founding member Brian Jones, whose battles with numerous personal demons and plunge from the top mirror Jimi's rise and fascination with the drug culture.

As the Jimi Hendrix Experience gains recognition, Jimi's past associations throw their own stumbling blocks in his path. Contracts signed by him as a hungry studio session musician surface. Jimi's management team are able to put out most of these fires, but one particularly sleazy New York record producer refuses to be bought out, and even goes so far as to send a couple of Brooklyn wiseguys to London to bring back his artist.

Chasing Jimi is "The Sopranos" meets The Beatles. The author's intense admiration for Jimi Hendrix, his own magical experiences as a hippy in the great Summer of Love and a stint as a touring rock 'n' roll photographer in the 70s served as inspiration for Chasing Jimi.

Knowing the scrutiny he would be under for daring to write a fictional piece about Jimi, the author strived to be as accurate as possible in the timeframe of events. Liberties were taken, but they were taken in order to craft what hopefully is an amusing and entertaining tale that transports the reader back to a better time.

"Did you miss the 1960s? This funny, yet loving and respectful adventure mystery about the decade's electric sugar stud will take you back."

— JERRY HOPKINS, AUTHOR OF *THE DOORS: NO ONE HERE GETS OUT ALIVE.*

TINSEL TOWN: ANOTHER ROTTEN DAY IN PARADISE

"Tinsel Town is the best introduction-to-Hollywood novel I've ever read."

— DAVID GILER, PRODUCER/WRITER *ALIEN*, *UNDISPUTED, MYRA BRECKINRIDGE* AND MANY MORE.

A Hollywood novel by an author who has been there - done that. Jim Newport is an Emmy-nominated production designer of both film and television. His experiences in the early years of his career served as the inspiration for Tinsel Town.

Memoirs from those in the film trade are nothing new. The bookshelves are crowded with star biographies—directors, writers and producers offering to show how difficult and arduous it is to either direct, write or produce a movie. But Tinsel Town is no simple straightforward autobiography. Like Chasing Jimi, it is a work of 'faction' - combining fact and fiction. Tinsel Town doesn't gloss over the cracks in the scenery —the grit, the stench, the plain old-fashioned blood and sweat that making movies was really about in the wild and woolly Easy Rider days of independent filmmaking. A non-stop party.

Art student Joey Morton arrives in Hollywood in 1968 and stumbles onto a sound stage. It was everything a young New Yorker could possibly hope to find—sex, drugs, gorgeous women, backstage passes, access to movie stars, rock 'n' roll… and more sex and drugs.

The author not only gives the reader a glimpse into what it

was like to enter this privileged profession in arguably its most exciting time (when movies played out in front of your own star-struck eyes, rather than against a green screen to be digitally composited later), but he also spins a tale, unravels a mystery, and takes the reader on an adventure.

"Newport's novels succeed in their purpose ... they entertain."

— THE NATION.

"It moves like a runaway asteroid." Tim Hallinan, bestselling author of the Poke Rafferty series (set in Bangkok).

— TIM HALLINAN, BESTSELLING AUTHOR OF
THE POKE RAFFERTY SERIES (SET IN
BANGKOK).